A Wordsmith's Opus

A Wordsmi

Angela C

Copyright© 2023 Angela Craddock

All rights reserved

ISBN: 9798385939039

A Wordsmith's Opus

Author Biography

Angela Craddock lives in the North East of England with her partner Anton and their fox terrier, Teddy. She greatly enjoys books, foreign travel and cooking as well as spending time with family and friends. Her love of reading has been a lifelong passion along with a burning desire to be a writer. She founded The Buddies Book Club in 2013, bringing together a

collection of friends who share a love of reading. All of those original members are still enthusiastic participants. She views reading as a way of broadening the mind; stories are gifts to us from authors who share observations from their unique perspectives. She finds writing to be a cathartic process of self-expression and an interesting forum that entertains her readers. After working as a qualified nurse in the NHS for 35 years she has gained a wealth of experience and feels privileged to have helped her patients through every stage of life's bittersweet journey.

She is educated to degree level having achieved a Bachelor of Arts degree in Nursing Practice and a Postgraduate Certificate in Infection Prevention.

Following her retirement in 2020 she is delighted to have published her first book, 'Rookery Heights' followed by 'A Wordsmith's Medley', a short story collection. Her best ideas spring to mind on breezy walks along the coastal path between Whitley Bay and Tynemouth.

She is living her best life and has stopped waiting for Friday!

Email: angelacraddock22@gmail.com

Twitter: AngelaCraddoc12

Instagram: craddock.angela

Facebook:/angela.craddock.5

Special Acknowledgements:

To Anton Davidson, for always standing by me and being my right-hand man and to **Teddy** for being the best little dog

To Eve Smith, the kindest and best Aunty who I'm very lucky to have

To Julie King, my dear cousin and dedicated fan of my stories, thank you for always supporting me.

To all the members of my Buddies Book Club : Patricia Taws, Diane Rutledge, Lisa Wood, Sandra Sandy, Stephanie Hannant, Judith Pike and Veronica Holland. Thank you for your on-going support.

To Dawn Wilkinson, my kind, inspirational friend without whose help none of this would have been possible. I'm so grateful, thank you!

To all of my friends who follow me and support my writing, please know how thankful I am!

Dedication:

To Gladys Smith, my wonderful Mam. Thank you for everything, for your enthusiasm for my stories and loving me as you do. You mean the world to me.

Contents

The Deed Hoose	Page 8
Right Beside You	Page 11
The Other Side of You	Page 20
Road to Nowhere	Page 23
Death Threads	Page 29
Tycoon's Lagoon	Page 39
The Whispering Tree	Page 44
A Past Life Present	Page 53
The Extraordinary Talent of the Zancigs	Page 72

The Deed Hoose

Lizzie Griggs was always dressed in a thick coat and she scuttled along the fish quay beach like a black scarab beetle. With her little round spectacles and gold earrings that dragged slits in her ear lobes, she was well known by all the local folk. She had been married once but now lived 'over the brush' with a ferryboat man. This was considered to be shameful though no-one voiced their opinions on the matter.

In blazing sunshine or freezing blizzards she monitored whatever washed up, though not in the way that a beachcomber searches for driftwood or sea-glass. Lizzie retrieved dead bodies that were returned to shore. Whether through high spirits or depression, accident or inebriation, they shared the same watery fate. Sometimes, at high tide the rip currents could easily drag men into the black Midden waters.

Drunken seafarers who lost their footing whilst clambering over vessels were engulfed by the swell. Some were deliberately pushed into the River Tyne following a fight; these victims of foul play stood little chance of redemption. Bodies that drowned at Cullercoats, Whitley Bay or further north would also wend their way here, bloated, ravaged by crabs and decomposed.

Although Lizzy was small in stature, she was incredibly strong. She transported the deceased to the mortuary in a decrepit, pull-along cart. It did not afford any dignity but provided a practical solution to a transfer problem.

The Deed Hoose stood on the quay at Clifford's Fort, next to a smokehouse. It was the designated holding place for any washed-up corpse. The building was squat and built of blackened sandstone. Inside there was a lead lined slab with a sink at the bottom and a washing trough with hose. Though only crudely equipped, it was refrigerated, at least. Crates of beer and boxes of fish were stored right next to the instruments that performed the post-mortem operations.

The long summer days attracted children, much to the dismay of the police officers who patrolled the quay. It was an unsafe playground which offered derelict hiding places and the potential for mischief.

One afternoon Lizzie was keeping watch when she noticed something unusual. A greyish shape was washing in, which she assumed was a dead seal or dolphin. She was shocked to see it was the body of a boy. Even though she was hardened by the repetition of her job, a tear escaped from her eye as she lifted him into her arms and carried him to the Deed Hoose. There was nothing else to be done. His eyes stared blankly and his limp limbs flayed. A member of the

River Police who had been out searching for him responded to Lizzie's shouts.

She laid the lad on the slab. He was declared dead and covered with a blanket. A couple of hours later his grandfather came to identify him and was then led away, distraught and weeping.

Lizzie stripped the lad and briskly sluiced his body with the hosepipe. Suddenly he began coughing and spluttering. Lizzie cried, "Quick, this laddie's alive, get the doctor to him! There's no place for him here in my Deed Hoose!!"

Right Beside You

Jonno Holloway loves motorbikes and lives his life in the fast lane. He has chosen this as a lifestyle, not to be bad-assed or rebellious, but for the freedom and excitement that it affords. He is a member of The Blazing Bandits Biker Club which gives him a sense of belonging, yet he projects individuality in his personal appearance and in his choice of mean machine. He is stockily built, not fat, but large and muscular. Jonno looks like a tough guy but underneath his bandana he has crinkly eyes that smile. The hair that is lacking on his head grows abundantly into a salt and pepper coloured beard. His girlfriend Evie is blonde and petite with a winning smile. She has to compete for time with Jonno and sometimes feels she is not the first love in his life, or even *a love* of his life, but she loves him. Today she won't see Jonno as she's having a spa day at Mount Royal Hotel, a Christmas present from her sister.

Jonno considers that people are like motorbikes in that each is customised a bit differently. The idolisation of two wheels is literally his driving force and one that nurtures his soul. He adores his faithful road companion, respecting its power and agility. He rides all year round; the summer days when he feels the wind on his face are the ultimate, although harsh weather presents no obstacle. He believes that life is not about waiting for storms to pass but about learning to ride in the rain. If you don't ride in the rain, you don't ride and that would surely be lousy.

He is a thrill seeker, an adrenaline junkie whose body floods with endorphins when travelling at high speeds, hence his addiction to the high risk pastime. Today is perfectly dry and sunny and he can't wait to zip up his leathers and go. In the garage stands the Kawasaki Ninja, his four cylinder pride and joy. He pats the seat and strokes his hand over the cool, shiny paintwork that he keeps in immaculate condition. The main frame of the bike is white, a Japanese Toryu *dragon slayer* is emblazoned on the side. Lime green flashes at the front and rear with red 'tick' shaped features add to the overall striking appearance. At the push of a button the garage door automatically raises, he pushes his bike out and dons the rest of his kit. His head protection is a top of the range Arai helmet as he likes to keep it all Japanese. He knows that some of the highest profile motorcycle racers favour the brand, and safety can't come with too high a price tag. Steppenwolf pops into his head and he can't help but sing, "Get your motor runnin', head out on the highway....we can climb so high, I never want to die". He is ready to roll.

This is what it's all about, Jonno thought, two tonnes of steel and some padding between him and the road. The engine's at full throttle and he's streaking down the carriageway; man and machine have morphed into one. He has already passed some members of the brotherhood who have given him the biker wave, and he has acknowledged and returned the gesture, *'keep two tyres on the ground and stay safe'*. It makes him feel like a modern day knight, with horse, armour and a special code of honour. The road evokes many sensations for Jonno; sweet memories, smells of nature and feelings of euphoria. He particularly enjoys blasting down this stretch of road before he starts slowing down for the seafront approach. Coming up is a very tight, blind bend which he must prepare for, before he reaches the caravan park. On the other side is the cemetery and he's not planning on going there any time soon, so he reduces speed and leans into the curve as he has done countless times before. Today there are scattered grass clippings strewn across the road, blown there from a private access road to a farm. He cannot safely switch lanes and the bike loses traction on the slippery vegetation, causing him to swerve and lose control. The bike skids and scrapes along, eventually keeling over at its resting spot, less damaged than Jonno is soon to be.

Now he finds out what it is like to fly, as he becomes a separate entity to his bike, hurtling through the air before hitting the ground with a sickening thud.

Blackness is all he knows as his crumpled body lies there and his brain is stunned by the shock of his fall. Then he hears a voice shouting, "Jonno, dude, come on, come on, look at me, you gotta open your eyes". He cannot respond, he's locked into a private dark place that he has never known before. Someone is shaking him and shouting, "Breathe, come on you gotta breathe, man." Jonno becomes aware of a pin prick of light that is getting larger and looks like the round opening of a tunnel. He feels a sensation of warmth radiating through him and he tries his very hardest to open his eyes to confirm what he already knows to be true. His little brother Robbie is there with him.

Everything is fuzzy but through the blur he can make out that it is Robbie. "Bobster!" Jonno barely croaks, using the childhood nickname he bestowed on his youngest sibling. Bobster's huge face is illuminated by the brightest rays of dazzling sunlight. More shaking, more shouting cannot stop him from drifting away to a peaceful place of beauty and serenity. His desire to experience more of this wonderful place is overwhelming. "Come on, breathe, you're gonna be ok, Jonno, I know it, but you gotta breathe," shouts Bobster.

Caroline is on her way to work and carefully negotiates the on-coming bend, as she always does. She is shocked to see a bike without a rider lying in the crest of the road. As soon as she sees a man slumped on the verge she pulls over, puts her hazard lights on and leaps from her car. Down on her knees and with her head close to Jonno's face she quickly establishes that he is not breathing and she can detect only the weakest thread of a pulse. With years of experience as an A&E nurse she knows exactly what to do, but she is filled with trepidation at having no equipment or back-up. She calls out to an approaching man who is already on his phone to get help, to ring 999 for a paramedic ambulance and police. She starts chest compressions, Jonno's partially digested breakfast spurts forth from his mouth. She keeps on resuscitating, even though it's hard on her back, and her knees, she goes all out to give this man a chance. After what seems like an eternity, but was actually six minutes, she is relieved to hear the emergency service sirens. The attending police officers quickly assess the scene, set up a road blockade and make conditions safe. The sirens and flashing lights increase as more responders reach the scene. They start a collision report and take measurements and photographs of the accident scene.

Two paramedics come rushing to her assistance with a full equipment kit and automated external defibrillator. One takes over with the chest compressions, the other cuts open Jonno's leathers and rips his favourite T-shirt then applies the sticky electrode pads to his chest. The automated defibrillator voice declares, 'Do not touch the patient, analysing rhythm, shock advised, charging, stand clear!' The electric shock is delivered, it jolts like lightning through Jonno's body, his arms flail about then fall to his sides. A heart trace is now visible on the monitor; Jonno's heart is beating again. "Come on bro,

you can do this, hang in there, you'll be ok," shouted Bobster.

The paramedics work together to insert an IV cannula and to intubate. His neck must be immobilized with a hard collar before he is moved. They are going to take care of Jonno's airway and breathing to help get him through this crisis. Once they have secured a tube in his airway and stabilised him as much as possible, they scrape him from the ground and slide him onto a stretcher. One of the paramedics checks to see how Caroline is and thanks her for the life-saving efforts. She tells them she is on her way to the hospital, as it's her place of work. She will try to catch up with them in the Emergency Room. The paramedic checks the scene to see if anything is left behind and suddenly remembers the chain he removed from Jonno's neck.

Discarded in the grass was the skull pendant, a biker's talisman. Jonno is never seen without this; it is a symbol of immortality and a guardian angel's protection from death. It's inscription, ever poignant to Jonno reads, 'Live to ride, ride to live', and he tucks it safely into his pocket until he can return it to his patient.

"Jonno, I'm still here, I'm coming with you! Hold on in there buddy, you're a fighter," shouted Bobster. The ambulance doors slam shut and they set off to the hospital at top speed, with blue lights blazing.

In Emergency Room T1 the staff were prepared, waiting to receive their casualty. They took over Jonno's care and attached him to the cardiac monitor. "Great job, guys!" says leading trauma Doctor Jensen in praise of the paramedics. "Blood pressure is high and heart rate slow but he's still with us. We'll get him to scan, let's see what's going on in his head."

Just then Jonno felt an incredibly strong force pulling him out of himself, disconnecting him from his physical body. He levitates above himself, floating higher and higher until he is trapped by the ceiling. Looking down he sees the nurses hovering around him, checking his observations and taking bloods. He sees Dr Jensen's bald patch that's right on top of his head. He can see Bobster in the corner of the room, also watching the proceedings. Jonno had never experienced anything like this before; he is outside of his own body. Oh God, am I dead, he wonders? No, that just can't be so. Suddenly the nurses are acting urgently, attaching him to the defibrillator again, injecting drugs and fluids into his veins. Bobster has both hands over his face but is peering through his fingers. None of it makes any sense to him. On the ceiling a film show plays, in which Jonno takes the starring role. A frame-by-frame record of life events is showing. It's all about him, snapshots of his life flash before him at a ridiculous speed, birth to 38 years depicted in seconds. All of his happiest times are replayed before him and he feels immersed in feelings of peace and dissolution. The defibrillator delivers a further shock and he is sucked back into his body, hurtling in with brutal force.

"He's back with us!", says Dr Jensen with relief. "Let's get him to critical care once we're happy with his vital signs."

Jonno is transferred to the Intensive therapy unit for continuing care and observation. He moves in and out of consciousness and has no concept of time or place. The machines that are supporting him constantly chime out their annoying alarms. He cannot open his eyes due to swollen sockets but a Staff Nurse periodically prises open his lids to shine in a light. At such times he sees her blurred blue uniform and not much else. His Mam and Evie have been sitting with him, willing him to get better and he recognises their familiar voices though he cannot respond. The days roll into nights and he slowly begins to improve. The brain swelling has gradually reduced though it will take weeks for his broken bones to heal. Today they are going to switch off the sedation and carry out a neurological assessment. Maybe they will be able to remove the breathing tube that connects him to the ventilator, then he will hopefully be able to talk again.

"Ok, let's get him extubated," suggests Dr Jensen. They sit Jonno up and remove the tube, suctioning out the saliva and secretions and he coughs and coughs. An oxygen mask covers his nose and mouth. His raspy weak voice says, "Get Mam... Evie, wanna speak to them!"

They are brought to his bedside; they stand on opposite sides, each holding his hands.

The nurse briefly moves his mask to one side and he uses every ounce of effort to say, "Where's Bobster? I've seen him, he's been with me all the time, waiting by my bed!"

The visitors exchange looks of shocked puzzlement. They don't know what to say or indeed how to say it.

Jonno's Mam has tears running down her cheeks and with great difficulty she leans in and says, "Jon, I think you are a bit mixed up, have you forgotten... that Robbie... is no longer... with us? Drugs got the better of him. You do remember he died of an overdose two years ago, don't you?".

Jonno looks totally bemused and emotionally states, "But Mam, he is right beside you. His hand is resting on your shoulder!"

The Other Side of You

Every day I live with a pain that is almost unbearable. I say 'almost' for I'm still here, still functioning, albeit in a very dampened down sense of being 'alive'. Existing, only just. There is no pleasure for me, my broken heart keeps beating, as full of love as ever it was, but it cannot sing, or burst with pride as it did before.

Josh, my brown eyed boy, my creation of perfection, my everything is gone. The memory is too terrible to recall, I try so hard not to think of it, but how can you shut out the sound of your visceral scream that emanates from deep inside? You cannot bury a memory so abhorrent; its intrusive infiltration is impossible to block.

Through the frosted glass I saw two blurred figures in dark clothing. Two police officers, one female, one male. I thought, surely not. Josh had only just left for school, swinging his bag over his shoulder, his laces not tied properly, unruly brown hair flopping over his eyes.

Their expressions reflected the seriousness of the news they had to deliver.

"Mrs Jenkins?" they enquired, "This is PC Blacklock and I'm DS Perry. Can we go inside?" they requested.

They asked me to sit down. I braced myself. You have the wrong person!

"I have some very bad news to tell you. Your son Joshua has been involved in a road accident", then pausing before the crucial, life changing punch, he continued," I am sorry to have to tell you he has died."

Disbelief washed over me and I said, "No, you've got that wrong, officer. Not my son, he will be in school now", I assured them, shaking my head, emphasising just how wrong they were. That is how I found out that Josh had been hit by a car on the pedestrian crossing. A newly qualified driver displaying the 'P' sign failed to stop for the red light. My son smashed onto the bonnet, flung upwards before crashing down onto the road, striking his head. Too severe an injury for a boy to sustain, he must have been killed almost outright, lying crumpled in the road like a broken toy.

"I saw the car coming towards me, a male teenager behind the wheel, not slowing down, no time to stop. No time to think or run, it happened so fast, and yet so slow. The force of the collision flung me in the air like a crash-test dummy, I bounced off the car then hit the road, couldn't open my eyes; the crushing blackness came and I knew no more. I was taken to hospital though there was nothing they could do but file me away in a freezing cold cabinet, my case closed. Please search for 'P'. Black car. RIP JJ".

Ten days later I sat in Josh's bedroom. His funeral now over, I was emotionally void and totally unprepared for what I found in the notepad, in his own writing, an accurate description of the fatal accident, his macabre, psychic premonition.

Road to Nowhere

The doorbell rang, well I wasn't expecting anyone and I grabbed a tea towel to dry my hands as I headed down the hallway. I could see two dark figures through the frosted glass and I opened the door without a thought or a care about security, or who they were, or what might happen if they forced their way in. One of them did show me their I.D badge, even though I hadn't asked to see it. You never think it's you that they want to speak to, even when your heart starts to beat just a little bit faster. Possibly a burglary or an accident in the street, a warning from Neighbourhood Watch to be on alert for youths running amok...

Are you Sarah Jenkins, she asked me and I slowly replied, yes...that's me. We are police officers from the North Yorkshire force. I knew that, I'd already worked it out as I heard their radios crackling. Not that their uniforms look as formal as they used to; it's all polo shirts, high 'vis' and stab vests these days. I'm PC Hollings, said the female officer, and this is DC Lewis, gesturing towards him. It's about your son, Daniel Jenkins, can we come in please?

So I stepped to one side to allow them to pass. Go through to the back, I told them. You say it's about Dan, is he alright? What's happened? By now my mouth was dry and it wasn't just my heart that was racing, but my mind was too. The tea towel dropped to the floor and

I trod on it on the way past. He is ok, isn't he, I asked, and my eyes flicked over both of their faces, trying to detect any giveaway sign, the slightest indication of how serious things might be.

Daniel has had an accident. He is in a serious condition and has been transferred to hospital for emergency treatment. He was driving a black BMW which skidded off the road and hit a tree. There was a young female passenger who was also taken to hospital. Then he stopped talking, I think to give me a chance to absorb what he had said. He doesn't have a BMW so how can that be, I asked, and he's just got himself an apprenticeship and passed his driving test, I added, as if any of that mattered. I warned him to be careful, to watch his speed. You know what young lads are like when they get behind the wheel. The officer gave a measured, ironic smile because he knew only too well what I meant. We certainly do, he said.

Was he conscious, I mean, talking or anything, and he said no, not talking but he was breathing. Ohh well, that's something, isn't it? I said rather optimistically, then realised how foolish that must sound, because breathing is such a basic requirement for being alive and it barely translates as good news. Then he went on to say that the road was currently closed and the area had been taped off, they were taking measurements and photographic evidence, assessing the road conditions as part of the investigation. Whose car was it, who was he with, I asked. It must be his girlfriend, Laura, was it Laura? He couldn't tell me, we're awaiting formal identification, he said. Oh, no, let them be alright, I pleaded, and then the dreadful news started to sink in and my composure cracked, because until then I thought there had been a huge mistake, the wrong street, wrong person but now I realised this really was my drama being played out in my living room, about my son; it was about us after all. That's when the tears came. A single drop rolled off the end of my nose without warning. I don't like to express my emotions in front of others but I was taken off guard, and when you are given bad news out of the blue, it's only natural, isn't it. I don't know why I'm trying to excuse the fact that I cried, and it's not as if the officers haven't seen it all before. It was a terrible shock, I felt dazed and couldn't take it all in. He's not a bad lad, you know, he's got himself into a few scrapes before but nothing serious, just the usual stuff for lads of his age. I saw the officers exchange fleeting glances. I think there are a lot more questions than answers at the moment. We will know more in the coming days. Let's take you up to the hospital, he said. The female officer smiled and I saw sympathy in her eyes. Come with us and we will see how he is doing, she said and gave my arm a little, unexpected squeeze.

D.C Lewis pressed the intercom button to announce our arrival at the Intensive Care Unit then a member of staff came and asked us to sit in the quiet room. I noticed a box of tissues on the table, just waiting there to mop up the next round of bad news. A few minutes passed though it seemed much longer, then a nurse appeared. Hello, I'm the nurse in charge, she said, but she looked so young I couldn't believe it really, that she could have enough experience for that sort of responsibility. Are you Sarah Jenkins, she wanted to know, so I said yes, I'm Dan's Mam. He is going to be alright, isn't he? She sat down next to me on the small sofa and was close enough that I could smell her perfume and see the strand of hair that escaped from her neat bun. She was a pretty girl, her eyes were kind. "Mrs Jenkins, Daniel's condition is serious, he is stable at the moment but that could change at any time. He has a hard collar in place which is supporting his neck, in case of spinal injury, there are quite a few cuts and bruises. He is connected to a breathing machine, a ventilator. The machine is doing all of his breathing and we gave him some strong painkillers to send him off to sleep, to allow the machine to do the work. He is attached to a heart monitor and he has a tube in his wrist which gives us a constant recording of his blood pressure. When you come to see him I will get the doctor to explain the results of the CT scan which was done to check out his head injury. It's a worrying situation and I wanted to tell you these things to prepare you, as it can be a shock when you see all of the equipment for the first time. Just remember it's all there to help him through this and we are doing everything we can. Do you want to see him? I'll take you down when you are ready".

It was late evening by now, on one of those autumn days that never seems to get properly light. Dan was in the third bed we came to but I had wandered past because there was nothing recognisable there to make me stop. He is back here, the nurse indicated. I don't think I was at all prepared for what I saw, despite the chat we had which was supposed to set the scene. He was somewhere in the middle of all that electrical equipment, the blinking, bleeping technology. It's ok, you can hold his hand, the nurse said, so I did. In the half-light I noticed his punctured veins with their inflamed track marks and I knew then that my suspicions were true. Now I could see how pale and thin he was, but how could he do such a thing to himself, how had this happened and why hadn't I asked him if he was in trouble?

Then I got a text from Laura, asking if it was true that Dan was in hospital after an accident and I knew that things didn't add up. The nurse shone a light in his eyes to see if his pupils reacted and the doctor told me that his brain was swollen. They would stop the sedation in the morning to assess how he was doing. They hoped to see some improvement over the next few days. There's nothing you can do tonight, they said, you need to go home and rest, so I did.

PC Hollings came back to see me. Investigations were ongoing but this is what was known so far. She believed that a dealer had offered Dan some drugs for free, one dose of heroin is potent enough to cause immediate addiction. Once you experience that euphoric hit, you have to feel it again. He'd been drawn into a dangerous world and once trapped was forced to store and supply drugs for his unpaid debt. County lines runner, that's what it's called, and this was a foreign language to me. He'd stolen a car to get away from the ringleader, at the same time dragging a vulnerable girl off the street who he rescued from danger. He'd tried to save her but it was the devastating injuries sustained in the crash that sealed her fate. The lifeless body of the fifteen year old was taken straight to the mortuary.

Dan's first words to me were, Mam, what's happened, and I said well you tell me, son, but not just yet. You have another chance to live your life right, to get off the road to nowhere and I will make sure you do.

Death Threads

Secreted away in an underground research department of one of Britain's largest museums is a mummy vault. It's a world that is hidden from the public, a room of the fragile dead who lie on racks in carefully regulated temperature conditions. In 3,400 BC they walked this earth, existing in the hot, arid climate of Egypt; their civilisation has been a source of eternal fascination.

Dr Greta Rowan, professor and faculty curator of Egyptian Archaeology heads a team whose passion for research in this speciality is unquestionable. The memory of a visit to a museum as a child has remained with her, and the mummy she saw there ignited the spark of 'Egyptomania.' To Greta, this is not simply a job, it is a passion and obsession. She is knowledgeable and much respected by her team of experts including Sunil Sitaram, Ramesh Vanti and Lauren Fox.

They will soon be involved in an exciting new project and are preparing for the arrival of an esoteric exhibit. Excavated from the fortress town known as 'Area Z', 280 km west of Alexandria; a mummy of great historic importance is en-route to them.

The area is thought to have been supplied by transport barges from the Nile Delta where maritime traders carried olive oil, wine and opium. Spindle whorls and bowls associated with spinning of linen have been found where flax was cultivated. The team is assigned to studying urban and funerary remains and together will open the sarcophagus found deeply buried in sand.

Before they do so, Radiologists will carry out X-rays and investigation by CT scan to produce detailed images of the preserved human remains. They hope to learn more about life, society and culture from their findings. The team chatted about what they already know of the embalming procedure performed in a designated tent known as 'ibu'. The body was cleansed with palm wine then washed in water from the River Nile. The brain was removed by hooking it out through the nose and some other organs were removed, but never the heart. The body was covered with natron then laid outside for forty days to dry. Once all the moisture was removed, further cleansing with aromatic oils and resin took place prior to bandaging.

There is lively conversation in the coffee room and the team feel greatly privileged to touch the body and connect with its ancient past. Their excited anticipation is tangible. Greta's team is assembled and ready to receive the sarcophagus. They all wear protective gloves, masks and aprons and try to prevent any cross contamination from the laboratory environment. There are goggles too, but no-one wants to wear them as they mist up. They don't want to miss a second of this most unique reveal. Firstly they admire the elaborate paintings on the sealed sarcophagus, the outer container to protect the body from scavenging animals and tomb raiders. The coloured designs of the goddesses Isis and Nut look surprisingly bright and well preserved on the casing. Next they insert small, wooden wedges very carefully into the seam, easing it at both ends. The lid lifts cleanly off to reveal the coffin nestled inside, then the mummy wrapped in ornate linen can be seen. A musty aroma fills the room, not as unpleasant as you may think an ancient corpse might smell, though not particularly pleasant either. The scent is akin to mouldy bread with undertones of pine resin. Small particles of sand and dust become airborne, the motes are visible in a shaft of light. They all wondered if the elaborate rituals had successfully facilitated the soul's safe passage to the Duat, the afterlife?

The bandage mesh could clearly be seen, a type of four thread linen manufactured by a variety of techniques. Workers spun the flax fibres into thread which was woven on a loom. Greta wondered whose hands had performed the wrapping process which took one to two weeks to complete. Linen was a valuable commodity used for clothing, bedding and blankets. When it became worn it would be kept specifically for mummification. Hundreds of yards would be used to individually wrap fingers and toes; mummia glue was used then a protective binding shroud was applied. Sometimes material of finely darned silk threads was used to wrap the body, denoting a wealthy person of higher social standing.

Charms have been found wrapped between the layers, believed to have magical, protective powers and the team hoped to find textual amulets which are short magical spells. Papyrus was used as a form of stuffing; tax documents and even royal decrees have been previously deciphered by experts. Personal messages expressing hopes for the future and concerns about finance resonate with all humans through the ages.

The team believes that this is the body of a priest who lived in the third or fourth century. He appears to be aged between thirty to forty years at his time of death and this may have been brought about as a result of trauma. The team hopes to gain more information on the cause of his demise. Within the casket they discover manuscript messages from The Book of the Dead, funeral prayers and other writings which will be deciphered by experts in that field.

Sunil discusses with his wife, Sruthi, what it was like when they viewed the mummy for the first time. They often find themselves discussing his work over their evening meal which does not usually detract from their appetite. Sruthi is proud of her husband's academic achievements and that he has remained so passionate about Egyptology. Tonight she asks him if he is alright: she thinks he looks tired and he has eaten less than usual. Sunil denies feeling unwell but says he will go to bed a little earlier in preparation for a busy day tomorrow. The process of itemising their findings will get underway and Sunil needs to prepare and present a report on what they have elicited so far.

It takes a while for him to fall asleep, and when he does he experiences a recurrent dream. He is back in Alexandria on a field trip, an event which did actually happen, and he is walking near the Nile River Delta. The August sun is beating down and the river is high at this time of year and prone to flooding. This is seen as a blessing in such a naturally arid place. A casket washes up on the sandbank and he smashes it open, not something he would ever consciously do. Inside there is a skeleton lying in putrid, brown sewage water and the stench is horrendous. Sunil suddenly awakes, dripping in sweat and retching. He rushes to the bathroom, arriving there just in time as the rising yellow vomit spurts from his mouth. After a few minutes he brushes his teeth and takes some sips of water before returning to bed. The shivering starts, hot and cold, teeth chattering now, he feels ghastly. Sruthi has woken up and asks how he is, telling him he will have to phone work and take a sick day. Sunil grunts. His sickness record is impeccable, he will see how he feels in a few hours.

At 06:30 the alarm goes off as usual but the ringing goes on and on. Sruthi reaches across their bed and shakes Sunil to wake him but is unable to. His mouth is blue-tinged, he is breathing but is unresponsive. Sruthi is panic stricken, shaking and fumbling she rings 999.

At 09:20 Greta is already concerned that Sunil has not arrived at the museum. It is so unlike him and she wonders if there has been a public transport hold up. She sends him a text to see if he is alright but there is no reply.

In the Emergency Department the medics monitor Sunil's vital signs and his reduced level of consciousness. His condition continues to deteriorate and they pass a tube into his trachea to take control of his laboured breathing. They cannulate, they ventilate. Sruthi is really frightened as they try to stabilise him and is crying when she rings Greta to tell her of the distressing turn of events.

Lauren Fox is about to experience an incident at home when loading up her tumble drier. She tries not to use it very often, but she has a daughter, Amber, a messy toddler, and she finds that the washing quickly piles up. She needs to get a load dried this evening, so she stuffs the clothes in the appliance and starts the programme before carrying Amber upstairs. Amber loves her bedtime bath and story but sometimes Lauren is so tired that she falls asleep before reaching the last page.

In the utility room the dryer is becoming excessively hot; there is a smell of burning and the first wisp of smoke is emitted from the heating element which is thickly coated in fluff.

Lauren is awoken by the piercing sound of the smoke alarm at the top of the stairs. She can smell the acrid smoke and sees it seeping from under the door. She plucks Amber from her bed and carries her downstairs.

The tumble dryer bursts into flames. From the safety of the front garden, and trembling with shock she manages to dial emergency services.

Ramesh lives in south east London, next to one of the main tributaries of the Thames, the River Effra. He is interested in climate change and the recent predictions of drier summers and wetter winters in this part of the country. However, this August has been unusually wet and the soggy shoes, damp socks and umbrellas have not had the chance to dry out for days. The excessively heavy rainfall is a challenge for the parts of London which are still served by Victorian drainage systems. Underground rivers in the inner city often carry sewage overflow and have serious consequences. Ramesh has lived here for four years, not long enough to remember the last serious flood that occurred in Herne Hill, though his neighbours still talk about their appearance on the BBC national news. Last evening the local news station showed the rising river levels and discussed the potential consequences of the incessant rainfall.

The following day on his return journey from the museum he received two texts. The first was a severe flood warning from the Environment Agency. The second was from his neighbour, Tom, to say that their street was in a state of emergency as water had breached some of their properties. The sandbags Ramesh used to block his doorway had been totally ineffective. He knows that Category 3 'black water' contains pathogens that can make people severely ill, and rampant mould growth produces toxins which are also detrimental to health.

He puts his head in his hands. He has no idea how he is going to deal with this devastating blow.

Sunil has been transferred to a specialist Infectious Disease Unit. He remains in a chemically induced coma but is stable now and his tests have returned some interesting results. An expert in Epidemiology speculates that he has been infected by the Egyptian tomb bat, *Taphozous perforatus*, when particles of faecal pellets were released and inhaled. The Middle Eastern Respiratory Syndrome virus carries a thirty eight per cent mortality rate, though doctors tell Sruthi they remain hopeful for Sunil's recovery.

Greta has also received some news from the Hieroglyphics Team who have deciphered an ominous papyrus message; "Cursed be those who disturb this body. Those who break the seal shall meet death by fire, water and pestilence".

This project has been a total disaster, all of her team are absent from work, having befallen a range of catastrophes. She cannot accept liability for whatever else may happen in the name of research. Her responsibility to safely store, conserve and exhibit artifacts has never been greater, and she must question the ethics of the project with the Museum Director. Perhaps they should consider repatriation of the mummy, though that would incur further disturbance. The matter must be formally discussed with the Director and Chief Executive as soon as possible.

Lauren has called her insurance company and restorative work on the fire damage has started. Ramesh has also made an insurance claim for flood damage and is currently staying with a friend. Sunil has been taken off life support and has asked if Greta will visit him this evening.

The Museum's Strategic Board decided, for safety's sake, to close the case, literally. The coffin is to be returned to the sarcophagus, closed up and stored in a sealed vault whilst discussions on its ultimate destiny are decided upon.

It has been a very stressful time for Greta. She studies herself in the mirror, noticing the lines that have appeared around her eyes. She applies some makeup before setting off to visit Sunil. Once outside of the museum her phone starts ringing, so she answers, stepping off the curb straight into the path of a fast moving black cab. Her body is flung across the windscreen and then her head hits the ground, eyes staring wide in terror before a stranger brushed them closed for the very last time.

Tycoon's Lagoon

Greek shipping magnate Yannis Nicolaides stepped aboard his luxury mega yacht 'Celestial Sunstone' with his latest trophy wife decorating his arm. The 'silver fox' worked hard to maintain his physique; now aged fifty he was no longer as toned though still able to attract beautiful, young women. This *'zaddy'* uses his charisma, is well groomed and fashionable; women half his age lust after him and the lavish lifestyle he provides. His family is unfathomably rich, having taken advantage of an increase in the oil tanker trade in the sixties they managed to double their fleet. Located at the crossroads of ancient sea lanes in the eastern Mediterranean they are perfectly situated. It is not only tankers but bulk carriers, casino cruise ships and luxury yachts that make up their portfolio; they also own entire resorts in Dubai and modern art galleries right around the globe. Their riches are extremely mobile, largely tax exempt and their business offices reside in most capital cities.

Yannis's brother Theo stepped forward to greet them, kissing them both on the cheeks and holding on to his new sister-in-law's hand for just a fraction too long.

"Beautiful, isn't she?" Yannis rhetorically stated. "Fine bone structure and a lovely profile too," he added. "Anastasia has already attended her sitting with your artist. He has all of her proportions and will start the commissioned piece of work shortly".

"Excellent!" he declared. "Champagne is surely in order, let's celebrate your latest union and make a toast to our most extraordinary project! Santos, crack open an Armand de Brignac, would you?" he shouted. "She's just like the others, isn't she... with her long blond hair and sporty physique?" Theo winked at Anastasia when he thought he had caught her eye.

She quickly looked away, her face flushed with embarrassment and she felt of her depth. He was unable to detect the dismay in her eyes that were concealed behind dark designer shades. She hoped the conversation would spark off in a direction that she was no longer the focus of. The ice bucket arrived and she waited eagerly for Santos to pour her a glass. Many staff were employed to look after the Nicholaides and their guests, attending to their every need. They were highly paid to do so and had signed obligatory confidentiality contracts, a non-disclosure, *see nothing, hear nothing, say nothing* policy existed and any breach carried an extremely high cost.

Yannis jumped up to deliver the toast. "Here's to Mrs Nicholaides and to the success of our latest venture," Amphitrite Lagoon Underwater Museum.'

"Ee-gia mas....cheers!" and their glasses clinked together. "So, when do you think we will be ready to showcase our superb underwater art exhibition? The scuba diving and snorkelling school will experience unprecedented patronage; it will be such an awesome experience to explore the underwater sculptures. I can't wait to take a dive there! Life size statues modelled on real people who've been immortalised on the sea bed...it's an absolute stroke of genius and all credit to our wonderfully talented artist John-Felix Castillo!"

Anastasia quietly listened to their effervescent conversation. She watched the tiny champagne bubbles rising and popping and anticipated a refill.

"Do you dive, my dear?" enquired Theo.

Anastasia replied, "I am learning. I did the scuba diving just twice with Yannis, he is good teacher... but I do not learn it so fast," she replied, looking apologetically at her husband.

"You will learn all in good time. What greater incentive could there be, to see the exhibits first hand in their underwater environment?"

Anastasia fiddled nervously with her hair. She had not enjoyed the experience and despite Yannis's reassurance felt worried about what could go wrong. She had heard of divers getting trapped in nets, of equipment failure or shark attack. She really couldn't refuse, for she was beginning to learn that no one said no to Yannis. As Mrs Nicolaides the fourth she must overcome her fears. She was now living in luxury and had no desire to return to an existence of poverty in Russia.

John-Felix was keen to engage the locals in his gargantuan art project which would generate millions and make him famous. He asked them to model for some of his pieces, recreating their forms initially in cement. These life-size figures would then be submerged to the sea floor. In keeping with and reflecting the location there would be a sixteen feet tall exhibit of Poseidon, son of the Titans and his sea nymph wife Amphitrite seated in a chariot. It would weigh 60 tons and be technically very challenging to position. A colossal sum of money had been paid to him in advance and the rest of the funds would be transacted on completion of the project. His life would be changed forever as long as he managed to comply with all of the agreed specifications. It was too late now to back out, or to worry about the law, justice and morality. The refrigeration unit arrived in the dead of night, unwitnessed, and John-Felix prepared himself for the grisly task ahead.

Yannis became increasingly impatient and angry with Anastasia who did not want to scuba dive with him. She had turned out to be just as disappointing as the rest. He forced her onto the boat and into the water, determined that they would swim around the exhibits prior to the official opening. She was unaware that he had fitted her with the wrong sized mouthpiece and her cylinder had a faulty gauge.

They saw the figures standing eerily in a circle. The visibility was incredible and he clearly recognised some of the villagers. The chariot holding Persues and Amphitrite was magnificent; he must check that everything else was in order.

There they were! Tatiyana Nicholaides, Athina Nicholaides and most poignantly Petra Nicholaides, verily lapidified. They had annoyed him once too much, talked incessantly, spent too much. Now their fate was to keep each other company in stony silence, eternally encased in concrete.

The Whispering Tree

Mr Hedley is a bully, a repulsive characteristic in anyone, though especially a teacher. He is Head of Department for Physics at Morden High School, a position of power which he abuses whenever there are no witnesses. When he is not terrorising children in his class he has managed to seduce his colleague Mrs Mordue to partake in some extra-curricular activities of an adult nature. That also makes him a cheat and Mr Mordue so far appears unsuspecting of his wife's infidelity.

Fellow pupils Johnny Pikerley, Davey Fitzgerald and Benny Mason suffer the worst at the hands of Mr Hedley, so they try to stick together, whilst he tries his hardest to break them. None of the lads are very good at any subjects and Physics isn't anything that engages them. They can't answer any of Hedley's questions and are sitting targets for his ridicule, or worse still, deliberately inflicted injury, through his controversial teaching methods. As soon as the bell rings to announce the end of the school day Benny makes a run for it; being last out will invite trouble and a 'one to one' detention is to be avoided at all costs.

Tonight there is no cruel name calling, "Wet cheeto, rusty nut, ginger minger", Mr Hedley clearly doesn't have any time to waste here either.

Benny is a red head, he looks like a skinny whippet and his slight proportions are as a result of relative starvation. He runs fast until he is clear of the building. His Mother is an alcoholic who drinks most of the day and all of the night; her moments of lucidity are rare. There is no Dad on the scene, he has never featured in the lad's life. Benny has learned to take care of himself as there is no-one else to rely upon. Having no money and being hungry are the worst things so he has developed some survival skills; he is a petty thief, an opportunist housebreaker, a fridge raider. He is surprised at how many people leave their doors open, or top windows that only someone as slender and lithe as he could access. It fascinates and excites him to enter the homes of others, to touch their things and take whatever he fancies. It gives him a feeling of empowerment, and he can always think more clearly on a stomach that is not constantly grumbling.

Mr Hedley was telling a colleague that he was heading to the coast for the weekend. Benny overheard the conversation and noted it. He knows exactly where Mr Hedley lives and hopes he doesn't clear out his fridge before he leaves. It's the perfect chance to snoop around Hedley's home. He is going in!

Magda Shoreditch is seldom seen outside and cuts a strange figure in seventies style clothes from charity shops mixed with some hijab type clothing. Known locally as 'Mad Magda', Benny paid her a visit once. His curiosity was aroused when he peered through her letterbox, and when Magda's feet plodded upstairs he seized the chance to enter and explore.

So many people have lax security arrangements he mused, the door handle flipped quietly and with ease. His heart pounded in response to a sudden adrenaline rush. He entered the hall which was piled high with old newspapers. One room was just presentable, the one where her clients attend for sittings and psychic readings. Candlesticks, tarot cards and some sort of 'Monopoly' game was laid out on the dining table. A stuffed crow with glazed eyes was trapped pointlessly under a glass dome. Benny had never seen the likes before, darting from one room to the next he looked for anything that was worth taking. His eyes alighted on a £20 note under the mantlepiece clock and a pocket watch which he stuffed into his jacket just as the sound of her footsteps creaked on the landing. He ran through the kitchen, grabbing a chicken sandwich off the filthy bench before exiting into the garden. He stood in the shadow of a tree which was just starting to bud, though that's not what caught his attention. Hanging from it's branches was a single baby shoe, a dead squirrel in a tiny noose and a cat collar. Hoisting himself effortlessly he cleared the high fence but his baseball cap snagged on a twig and was left hanging on Magda's tree like an exhibit. Swearing under his breath at his carelessness he decided to leave it behind. This was preferable to being caught by the woman who at best is eccentric, or possibly mad.

Mr Hedley packed a holdall for the weekend. He would travel light for the train journey, a more anonymous form of travel in the circumstances. He didn't want anyone tracking his movements, noting his car registration, or worst of all, seeing him with *Gloria,* Mrs Mordue. He owns a caravan at 'Trees by the Sea' Holiday Park which would provide a secluded location for their illicit weekend. They will meet on the station platform with a taxi arranged for the last leg of the journey to the holiday site. Gloria has told her husband she will be attending a conference on a subject so dry and uninteresting that he thankfully didn't ask any questions.

Benny watches Hedley's house from a safe distance, waiting until the coast is clear. It's pretty much as he imagined it to be, not flashy but a well maintained, detached property on the outskirts of the village. He can't wait to get in there, to make use of the facilities, help himself to supper and smash a few things up. It's pay-back time for loathsome Hedley and nothing less than he deserves for the misery he has inflicted.

It's late afternoon as Hedley emerges, glances around and carefully locks the front door before leaving his property. He smooths down his comb-over hair. With an unusual spring in his step he sets off to the train station. Benny waits a while in case he returns, should he have forgotten something, such as closing the top window at the side of the house, the intended point of entry. Benny jumps on top of the wheelie bin and shimmies up, manoeuvring his skinny hips through the gap. On the inside window sill his foot catches on a Newton's Cradle, snapping the suspension wires and scattering the silvery ball bearings around the tiled floor. Benny remembered the time he was set up by Hedley to get a painful shock off the Van de Graff generator during a science demonstration. Evil scum of the earth!

What's in the fridge he wonders? The remains of a casserole, a block of cheese, a couple of beers, pizza in the freezer. Things are looking up, Benny thinks as he rips open a packet of crisps from the cupboard, stuffing them in his mouth as he continues his room-to-room surveillance. Through the patio doors he sees what looks to be a hot tub. Most surprising!

Suddenly there is a sputtering crack of noise followed by splintering, tinkling glass. In the hall stands a six foot tall pig wielding a pistol, or at least a man in a latex pig mask whose eyes don't match up with the holes. It would be funny if it wasn't so freaking terrifying.

"Get down on the ground, hands on yer head, do what I say!!" says the pig. Benny does exactly as instructed, best comply with his demands he thinks, or this could end badly.

"Who are you?" the man shouts, his voice is muffled by the mask snout.

"I'm, I'm err..B..Ben..ny"

"What are you doing here?"

"I broke in..."

"What for? Where's Hedley?"

"He's not here!"

"How do ya know?"

" He's away..for.. weekend".

"A conference?"

"Dunno..his caravan.. I think."

A few seconds pass before the realisation sets in, then the pig says, "So that's it, he's with my wife. I swear I will kill him." Suddenly, Mordue clutches at his chest and gasps for breath whilst sinking to his knees. His hand still holds the gun but his grip is loosening. He pulls off the mask, fighting for breath. His eyes are rolling, sweat dripping, he has a feeling of impending doom. He slumps forward, smashing his face in a terminal, bloody repose. No breathing now, no play acting, the man is dead! Benny is paralyzed with shock and fear. He is unable to think what to do next.

In his peripheral vision he sees movement; a figure dressed all in black and carrying a large suitcase. Benny is still crouched down, his erratic respiration was the only sound. The figure suddenly lunges at the corpse, grabbing the gun from his hand then pointing it at Benny's head.

The stranger says, "I've been waiting for this moment, you won't get the better of me. The voices told me you were here and it's been a while since I made them an offering; a sacrifice to my special, unique tree.

Now, here is a question for you to consider. Which would you prefer, death by gunshot or death by drowning? It's a hard choice to make. Maybe it's so difficult I will have to choose for you.

I want your life as compensation for a chicken sandwich, my father's pocket watch and a paltry twenty pounds. It's a high price to pay."

Magda was furious when she noticed the missing items. She was totally incensed that someone had hung a baseball cap on her tree. Only she could decide which items, which trophies should be selected as gifts to her whispering tree. She was sick and tired of mistrust and ridicule. Admittedly, the newspaper collections were out of control; too many missing people adverts to keep up with, countless tip-offs to the police who were seeking information and searching for them. If they had just listened to her, some of those people could have been found, even saved. The ladies used to come for their readings, looking for signs that would lead them to lost, loved ones. The messages were communicated to her in abundance back then. Simply holding a piece of clothing or jewellery would be enough to connect with that person and produce a vision of their whereabouts or sense of wellbeing. But the messages became weaker, her psychic visions blurred, inaccurate and the people stopped coming, stopped believing.

The tree voices told her to bring an offering, so Pussy-Willow was the first victim. The annoying cat that used her garden as its toilet marked the advent of something ominous. The strangled cat was buried under the tree and his collar was offered as a trophy. The squirrel was already dead but nevertheless served as a small contribution. After that her powers restrengthened and she was able to successfully locate the body of a missing toddler. She told the Police she had important information but they dismissed her as a time-wasting charlatan. Of course there was a shoe missing from the crime scene, she claimed it for herself.

The recent vision of Benny was a vivid one, clearly connecting him to Mr Hedley's property. Finding the location took concentrated effort but the rest came easily enough.

Crime Scene officers taped off Mr Hedley's house and garden and established his whereabouts. They confirmed Mr Mordue's identity and declared his death. A thorough investigation would take place and post mortem to determine the cause of death

which would appear in the first instance to be myocardial infarction (heart attack) followed by cardiac arrest. That would not, however, account for arterial blood spatter patterns on the walls and ceiling and absence of a murder weapon. They explore the possibility that a second victim was shot here then removed from the scene. Forensic samples will hopefully determine blood typing and DNA profiling.

Benny's broken body is stuffed in a suitcase at Magda's. Bodily fluids have begun to leak out and the stench is atrocious, though highly attractive to blue bottle flies. It is apparent he can't stay there much longer so Magda has gone in search of black bags, duct tape and a sturdy spade.

A Past Life Present

A darkened room lit with a dim night light, a hot milky drink and a bedtime story should be a restful way to end the day, but not for Amelia. She had always been a restless baby who was difficult to settle. Sleep still did not come easily and the visits in the small hours were a regular, unwanted disturbance. The child sat up and rubbed her eyes. It was happening again, a presence in the room. The door creaked open, the fabric of a long skirt rustled through the gap and the figure entered the room. "Why do you keep coming here? You frighten me," whispered Amelia.

Eliza's Story

I am Eliza Mahoney, I am 21 years old and I have recently secured a new and exciting position. I've been appointed as a nanny, tasked with the care of Master Thomas, the two year old son of Mr Thomas Carrington Snr and his good wife, Ida. They are a wealthy family; their descendants opened a small bakery business in Dublin. They told me that increased import of grain and maize became significant in the wake of the Irish Potato Famine and the earlier generations of Carringtons were in the right place at the right time, so they say. The business successfully grew and factory production was stepped up to meet the increasing demand for their savoury biscuits and oatcakes.

An opportunity has arisen to set up production in America, a lucrative deal has been struck with a company in New York and we are soon to emigrate there. Our tickets on a luxury trans-atlantic steamliner are booked and I am both nervous and excited at the prospect of my new life which beckons. We will be travelling first class and even my lively imagination cannot stretch to what that experience might be like!

The only suitcase I possess is battered, though the lid closes snugly enough. The leather handle is somewhat cracked but firmly attached. I hope I shall not be judged by it, or my few packed contents. I have some functional work dresses that could not be considered elegant or the height of fashion, however, they are *serviceable.* I shall put aside a little every month from my salary in order to achieve the look I aspire to. I don't wish to wear black every day and I hope it is not an expectation of my contract, something I must discuss with Mrs C.

Black is so dreary; it is a colour of mourning and doesn't allow self-expression. I shall buy some pastel pinstripe calico and find a fashionable dressmaker who can create me a professional look. In the immediate term I will have to make do with Aunt Orla's best cast-offs for which I am most grateful. She is an established entrepreneur in New York and It is she who has encouraged me to leave Ireland behind for a new life in America. She runs a chain of boarding houses which accommodate Irish immigrants until they establish themselves in the new land. Aunt Orla is kind, a philanthropist even, though no-one will take her for a ride or swindle her for she is sharp witted, so she is!

I was so excited to receive her last letter and gasped in wonderment when on opening, some banknotes fluttered to the floor. It was more than enough to feed our family for a week and yet it was all for me. *No niece of mine is travelling with an empty purse, and you must wear a hat and gloves when you disembark,* she stressed to me. I felt a wee bit guilty and will slip a contribution to Ma which will be a nice parting gesture. It's going to be really hard to leave them, there will be tears, but Da always told me I was a clever girl and I must set my sights high. He keeps tellin' me to follow my dreams so I'm seizing this chance because another one this good might not come my way.

I'm gettin' acquainted with Master Thomas now. I'm learning his likes and dislikes and what sets him off cryin'. He's a good little soul really, with blonde curls and a winning smile. He's got little pudgy knees and chubby cheeks and I like the feel of his arms around my neck. His clothes are fine and his shoes are exclusively handmade. He is privileged and knows nothing of hand-me-downs we have in our large families! I'm goin' to have to lay down the law or he will run circles around me and that won't please m'lady. She told me I'm doing a grand job so far, which was most pleasing to hear. In just twenty three days we will set sail from Queenstown and I'm counting down the days with both excitement and fear. I must tell ya of something queer that's happened and it's been most unsettling! The other day I met a stranger on the Strand Road heading into Cobh and he stopped me right in my tracks.

"You're dat lassie that's heading to America shortly, aren't ya?" he asked, his misty old eyes staring into mine.

"Now how would the likes of you know that?" I asked, trying to hide my nervousness, replying to him in a mocking tone.

"Auch, word gets around these parts, to be sure!"

"So what of it, if I am?" I said.

"Well I think ya should know I've had a dream, some might call it a *premonition*. Dat grand ship you're heading away on, it's goin' to sink right to da bottom of da ocean so it be only right that I should tell ya".

I was nonplussed but I walked on, my cheeks flushed pink and I didn't look back. There's a lot of folk in these parts who are superstitious; they don't like change and they don't want you to get on in life. Never set sail on a Thursday and not on a ship with a cargo of bananas, don't whistle on deck, always step on with your right foot, they say. Well bananas to the whole lot of them, it's just a load of bunkum!

It's such a big thing for a girl like me to leave her small village in County Mayo, and everyone who exists here, behind. Who would have thought it could be possible? Well no-one can stop me now, it's the chance of a lifetime and I'm going to grab it with both hands.

On 11th April in Queenstown, County Cork, the harbour of Cobh bustled with crowds and carriages, all with a sense of lively, animated purpose.

The town was the departure point and last port of call for the transatlantic liner before leaving on its maiden voyage. The great ship was so large that it had to drop anchor behind Spike Island. White Star Line tenders and other small boats delivered the luggage of some of the first-class passengers. One hundred and twenty three passengers would join the ship here, transported from the piers by tenders. Many of these passengers had attended morning mass at St Colman's Cathedral and as the vessel sailed away, the steeple at the highest point overlooking the harbour would be their last sight of Ireland. I chatted to a young lad who told me he was called Eugene. He was the piper who played Erin's Lament as we departed; those notes hung in the air around us. It was hauntingly poignant and overly sombre, I thought.

I joined the Carringtons as we toured the decks. I had never seen anything as luxurious, sumptuous or elegant and wished I could live in my cabin for the rest of my days. The walnut furniture was exquisite; there was a highly polished dressing table and washstand and Master Thomas's cot lay at the foot of my bed. I ran my fingers over the fixtures, thrilled that I should be first to touch such perfection. It took far longer to unpack the child's clothes than my own. I placed my hat box on top of the wardrobe and thought how grand it looked in such surroundings. Aunt Orla urged me to get one of good quality which would last, and I had enjoyed choosing it and carrying it home with me. It symbolised the transition from my old life to the one that lay in front of me.

I happily watched Master Thomas in his slumbers and a feeling of fondness for him washed over me as well as a sense of accomplishment that I had already made Ma and Da proud of me.

We dined that evening in the dazzling first class lounge. The white tablecloths hung with razor straight edges and the napkins were encircled with special ceramic White Star Line holders. The puzzling assortment of crockery and cutlery baffled me but I watched and then copied the implements Mrs Carrington selected. She knew I was out of my depth but she was smiling and I think I even detected her little wink of reassurance. It was an overwhelming dining experience but I delighted in trying an assortment of delicious new flavours and textures. Potatoes and soda bread are good at filling your belly but this was really somethin' else. I suddenly had to ground myself, remembering my servant status in the midst of such grandeur. I trusted that I would not sleep so soundly that Master Thomas's cries would fail to awake me.

There was no nursery on board so the next day Master Thomas and I walked around the deck, engaging with our fellow passengers. Some were walking their dogs there and Thomas would greet their pets with wide open arms, eagerly patting their heads, yet with gentle understanding. We played with a spinning top, bathed in the Turkish bath and when he became tired we returned to our cabin for a wee nap. It was such a carefree time and I felt so lucky to experience the glamour and panache of it all. For three days we made great progress across the chilly Atlantic.

Just before midnight on day four something terrible happened that thrust me into a chaotic whirlwind of life and death decision making for which I had no preparation, nor indeed did anyone else. I often think of that phrase, '*all in the same boa*t', as surely we were, though some passengers made good choices in order to survive and the fate of others was sealed by bad choices and what I can only imagine to be predestined kismet.

A seemingly innocuous bump followed by a shudder marked the beginning of the next chapter of my life. Initially I thought it to be of little consequence though the rest of the crossing had been uneventfully smooth. After a few moments I heard raised voices from Mr and Mrs Carrington's cabin and then the sound of their door clicking shut. It was none of my business to investigate where he was going but I did hear him say he wanted to speak to a crew member. I listened for his return but quite some time passed and then there were more voices in our corridor. There came a rapping on my door and when I opened it, to my surprise there was Eugene, the Irish piper, standing there apologetically. He must have remembered having shown me back to my cabin on the first day when I became a bit disorientated.

"I'm sorry to disturb you Miss, but I wanted to tell you we have a problem..."

"What's happening?" I asked as a feeling of unease began to creep through me. I suddenly remembered the old man on the Strand Road and his words of warning.

"We've struck an iceberg, Miss! They say this ship is unsinkable but I'm not so sure of that. Put on your warmest clothes, go onto the higher deck and await further instruction. I'll help you when you get there", he added.

"Holy Mary, Mother of God," is all I could say, "I need to tell Mrs Carrington of this!"

I knocked and at first there was no response, then slowly the door opened and there stood Mrs C with braided hair and wearing her nightgown. "The ship's hit an iceberg, I've been instructed to go to the lifeboats and you must get ready and come also!" I spluttered.

"No my dear, I'm sure you are mistaken! My husband has gone to find out what that bump was but I'm sure it was nothing of concern. I shall get dressed and go to find him. Stay in your cabin with Thomas and wait until I return".

So I went to my cabin and I lifted Master Thomas from his cot. I began dressing him in as many clothes as possible to protect him from the cold night air. His little arms stuck out stiffly from his sides due to all of the thick layers and he wore a bemused expression which reflected how I felt. I dressed myself warmly, removing a blanket from the bed and thought about what else I needed and could manage to carry. I looked out into the corridor for Mrs C but by now there was much activity as people bumped and pushed alongside and past each other. The air of non-urgency had since departed and I could wait no longer. I carried Master Thomas and a small bundle of possessions and we left our cabin for the lifeboat deck. "Thomas, we're going outside to look at the twinkly stars", I said as boldly as I could, and he smiled because he liked the sound of that. We made our way just two decks up and I was assessing the scene and deciding what to do next when I realised I'd left my precious hat behind! I simply had to go back and couldn't believe my stupidity at forgetting it, so we returned to our cabin and there was still no sign of the Carrington's. I shoved and jostled my way back to the upper deck and you will doubtless think that I was an eejit for giving up my place in order to retrieve my hat, until I tell you this. We were preparing to board lifeboat 5, a number that has previously proven unlucky to me. I just felt as though I shouldn't get in. Call it instinct, or gut feeling but I knew not to go then. As it was leaving there was a man with a shawl covering his head (poorly disguised as a woman) who jumped on board and in doing so capsized that very boat. I thanked my lucky stars that we hadn't gotten in. By now, lifeboat 11 was preparing to leave. That somehow seemed a more favourable number and a crew member helped us aboard. I looked for Eugene but was disappointed not to see him there, though it was hardly surprising in the midst of such panic and confusion. I took one last look at the ship and there on a lower deck was Mrs C who was screaming hysterically and being restrained by the crew.

"I will look after Master Thomas and do my best for him. We'll meet you in New York," I shouted into the blackness but my words were carried into the wind and I had little faith that I could keep my own frangible promise.

Amelia's Story

Everyone agreed that I was different and yet no-one could determine why that was. As a child I didn't feel the same as the others but of course, I only knew what it was like to be me. In a similar way that a blind person has little appreciation of the colour green I found my situation was very difficult to explain. I had neither the vocabulary nor the cognition to express myself. At times I was distracted by the other person that seemed to exist inside of me. One who selfishly demanded my attention, often pulled me awake from my dreamy state and mentally confused me as to what was real or imagined. I absorbed myself in childhood games, I was never alone as I chatted away, not to an 'imaginary friend' as most people believed, but to an entity that was very real to me.

I attended one doctor's appointment after another, clinics, surgeries, had tests and sleep studies and even a psychiatric referral. Whilst they all considered my unusual symptoms I remained trapped in my puzzling and scary existence.

My fear of water became apparent when I refused to even paddle in the sea. No-one could teach me to swim as my body stiffened with fear and the acoustic assault of my screaming was unbearable. I felt as though I couldn't breathe properly. My panic attacks became too difficult to manage and the upset and disruption they caused was better avoided. Try as they might, my parents did everything they could to help me as my problems became increasingly complex.

Hypnagogic hallucination...have you ever heard of such a thing? It's something that can happen in the transitional time between wakefulness and sleep. It can be a feeling of floating, spinning or falling, or that there is another person present in the room. You may sense an impending threat and I can tell you it's distressing. I would hear the rustling skirt and feel my mattress dip down as the shadowy figure joined me in bed. Then I would feel the fingers on my back and quiet breathing in my ear. I experienced what the doctors described as sleep paralysis where I was temporarily unable to move as my muscles went limp. I didn't mention to anyone that the visitations were not purely nocturnal.

The medics came up with differing theories and suggestions as to the possible cause. Was it cataplexy that I was suffering from, triggered by fear, they wondered. I heard them say that it would be nice to have a name for it, a diagnosis, and then a treatment plan which would hopefully improve things for me.

I was then referred to Dr Quigley, a Paediatric Consultant Psychologist with a special interest in people like me! I was fed up with doctors' questions and ahead of the appointment had already decided to say very little. When we got there I was surprised to be greeted by a lady with bouncing chestnut curls and a smiling face. Her dangling earrings danced around her face as she moved and her eyes were bright and engaging. Inside her consultation room there were toys in a box and brightly coloured bean bags to sit on. She shook my hand as if I were an adult and then offered me a sweet from a jar that stood on her desk. "I am Samantha", she said, "and I believe your name is Amelia. I want to help you."

She started off by chatting to Mum and I listened to all of the usual questions being answered with the same old responses. I can't really tell you what was different about that day other than I decided that I liked her. I liked that she was female as I'd seen so many stuffy, male doctors in foisty, tobacco-smelling suits. I felt unusually responsive to her friendliness and lack of formality. She flopped down playfully on a bean bag next to me and I felt able to tell her something that I had not previously disclosed.

I told her that just before my tenth birthday I made a groundbreaking discovery of a book at a church jumble sale. I came across it by sheer chance. As I studied the cover and flicked through the pages I was filled with feelings of deja vu and overwhelming familiarity. The pictures and photographs were acutely real to me, as if I had actually been there. The smells, the feel of the fixtures and fittings were tangible and I was flooded with a series of kaleidoscopic flashbacks. In that enlightening moment I came to accept the eerie notion of having lived before. It was time to tell my story now that things made more sense to me.

I told her that I had lived a previous life. It felt as though a restless spirit or soul had somehow become trapped inside of me, in my present life.

Her expression was one only of reassurance and concern. I saw sympathy in her eyes. I didn't detect any element of shock or recoil and she told me she had heard of such a thing. I was not the only one! She said I had taken a brave step and now she would be able to help and support me. If my parents consented, next time we would try some *hypnotic regression* and she gently explained what it would entail. It's a way of recovering repressed memories of a past life and she would make sure that I would feel comfortable and safe. The idea of it didn't frighten me, afterall I was used to living with my demons.

As you can imagine, my parents were shocked, even freaked out at my revelation, although I know they had their suspicions. They had surely discussed the possibility of me having had a past life, along with the other potentials of personality disorder, psychosis or schizophrenia. I wasn't mad or bad, I realised I was special because not everyone gets to live a second life.

Samantha made me comfortable and I began to concentrate on her steady, calming voice. Soon I felt drowsy and entered a transitional state where I was neither fully awake nor dreaming.

"You are now in a different life, a life that you have lived before, in a different time. What name can I call you by?"

I spoke for the first time ever with a soft Irish accent, introducing myself as Eliza Mahoney. Through hypnosis I was able to reveal the events of my past life story. The memories which had been forever 'locked in' now had a forum where they could be released. Eliza's words tripped from my tongue and my strong sense of connection to a certain era and place was about to be explained.

"Thomas and I survived the sinking of RMS Titanic, being rescued from the lifeboat and brought aboard RMS Carpathia. The terrors of that night haunted me for the rest of my days, my phobia of water after being lowered into an inky black sea amid the desolate screams of the doomed were always with me. There was a heart-stopping moment during the rescue operation, for there was only a rope ladder available to climb aboard the Carpathia. I had to place Thomas in a hessian mail sack so he could be hoisted up onto the ship. He was frightened and struggling and during that precarious transfer he very nearly dropped into the sea. I was tortured by recurrent nightmares, the sequence of events that night played over and over in my mind. I had promised to keep Thomas safe, the poor mite would surely be an orphan as his parents left it too late to board a lifeboat. I knew in my heart that they had perished and all I could do now was to look after Thomas as if he were my own. In fact, I managed to convince myself that I had actually given birth to him, and that little fella became everything to me, my whole world.

On 20th April we at last arrived in New York, docking at Pier 54. We queued at the White Star Line Offices where our names were added to the list of survivors. It did cross my mind to assume the identity of Mrs Carrington but I decided against it at the last moment. I was too traumatised and dehydrated to think it through properly. My Da's voice in my head told me to do what was true and honest. We were met by a scene of mayhem. Crowds of people had gathered, waiting anxiously for news of their relatives and there, pushing through the throng was the wonderful sight of my Aunt Orla".

She said, "My dear girl, I knew you were alive, I just felt it. I'm so happy to see you", and she wrapped her arms around the pair of us, crushing us with love. We all began to cry. Poor Thomas was confused and stretched out his arms to Aunt Orla. "Mama, Mama?" he kept saying to her. It was heartbreaking.

"No, my love, this is your Mama now", she said kindly, the sorrow for his situation reflected in her eyes. We were bedraggled, our only clothes were the ones we stood in. My battered hat perched on my head like a dead bird. I knew Aunt Orla would help us in every way she could, and I had never before felt more thankful. She wrote to my family in Ireland as soon as she could, to tell them I was alive and that I'd saved an infant who was now in my care.

We started our new lives, not in the way I planned, though in a revised, 'Plan B' kind of way. I cleaned the boarding houses, ordered supplies and Thomas stayed with me every step of the way. I loved that wee boy and if anyone enquired of his Da I told them the truth, that he had drowned at sea. Now that is what they call a conversation stopper. The fact he was not my husband thankfully needed no further explanation.

I felt desperately homesick when I chatted to the Irish immigrants who boarded with us, but of course, I couldn't return to Ireland. There was no way I could get on any ship ever again. So we stayed in America and made the best of our existence.

Some time later a sealed envelope arrived, addressed 'To Whom it May Concern". It was from a distant relative of the Carringtons who, having made contact with The White Star Line, were informed that Thomas was a survivor of the Titanic tragedy. I was instructed to contact a lawyer who was in receipt of documents outlining a trust fund for Thomas. Whilst I was overjoyed that he should inherit his family's wealth I was terrified that I might lose him, for that I could not bear. He was my whole world, my everything. I was extremely cautious when handling this matter, but as it turned out no-one was interested in taking Thomas from me. It was in his best interests to stay with me, so that he did. He was such a kind and well-mannered boy; I could not have wished for a better son.

The session drew to a close, Samantha slowly brought me out of my hypnotic state. My face was wet with tears and I felt drained by the experience but also strangely uplifted, having outpoured my story.

The Irish accent vanished, I was me, Amelia once again.

With the passage of time I was not as troubled by Eliza. It was as if she was stifled and not so actively present as before. I read up about survivor guilt which is experienced by someone who has survived a life-threatening incident where others died. Obsessive thoughts haunt the survivor who wishes they had done more to help others. I spoke to her, "Eliza, you did the best you could with your life and must let go of your negative emotions. You were a good person. I think your spirit is trapped, but you can go on your final journey now." I kept telling her to give herself credit for saving Thomas and to forgive his parents for remaining on board.

"It's time for you to be released from this world, go towards the light and onwards to a higher plane".

But Eliza still did not leave. It seemed there was only one final intervention, a very last resort. We asked for the help of an ordained priest, someone who was qualified to recite deliverance prayers to expel a spiritual entity. Though it is performed gently through prayers and blessings, the word 'exorcism' strikes fear in our hearts. Whether you believe in it or not, I am certain that it was this intervention that set Eliza free. There was a precise moment when I actually felt her leave me and I hope she shares my feeling of tranquillity as I live out the rest of this life without her. I have a strong sense that all is well now, as her spirit has transcended and her soul is resting in peace.

The Extraordinary Talent of the Zancigs

Julius Jorgensen smiled and extended his hand to the young lady, "Agnes, how thankful I am that our paths have crossed once more. I'm delighted to see you!" Julius could not hide his elation as he gazed into her eyes. He had often thought of her, especially in the last few months and was pleased that she was just as he remembered. As new immigrants they were reunited at a General Meeting held by The Danish Society. Agnes and her parents, Olaf and Ida left Copenhagen and had very recently arrived in America. Julius, his Mother Freja and Father Anton had embarked on the journey from Denmark to America ten months earlier, seeking a brighter future and freedom from oppression. In 1864 almost one fourth of Danish territory was lost when Slesvig-Holsten fell to Germany. Only the northern half of Selsvig was Danish so in southern parts military service became a requirement causing many Danes to flee their country.

Many of the immigrants were attracted by a certain incentive. Those who filed to become citizens could claim one hundred and sixty acres of unoccupied government land; they would build a homestead, work the fields and eventually make legal claim to the land under the Homestead Act of 1862.

The Jorgensens' situation was somewhat different. They had made a decent living at their iron smelting factory where Julius worked as an apprentice but were enticed by opportunity and adventure in a new land. They would continue in this line of work, on the assurance that extracting metals from ore in America would be a more lucrative proposition.

The Atlantic crossing took ten days, made considerably shorter by steamship, as previous crossings by sailing ship lasted on average six to eight weeks. For many, the journey was a treacherous one, not merely because of rough seas, but of crowded, unsanitary conditions in steerage which was rife disease. Some did not survive the journey and succumbed to a watery burial at sea.

The immigrants assembled here were the lucky ones, having arrived tired though otherwise unscathed. Their main focus now was to re-establish themselves and carve out a new way of existence in this foreign land. The purpose of the meeting was to welcome and support new members who were keen to keep alive a sense of belonging and cultural heritage of their homeland. A welfare fund was available for anyone suffering financial hardship or in need of practical assistance during the relocation period. Once all of the business discussions were complete there was the chance to socialise and make contacts. In the room next door a huge banquet was set out. A vast array of dishes were displayed on top of a table covering, a red cloth with white cross, the Danish *Dannebrog* national flag and patriotic bunting was hung from the ceiling.

There was pickled herring and shrimps on rye bread, frikadeller (veal and pork meatballs), puffed pancakes and kringle (almond pastries) washed down with beer and Aquavit snaps.

Julius and Agnes had lots to talk about, having not seen each other for many months. They were childhood sweethearts in Copenhagen but had gradually seen less of each other. Agnes's father had been instrumental in trying to separate them, determined that she would complete her education and achieve success. He had wanted something better for her than she wished for herself, the potential for early marriage to an apprentice foundryman.

With a friendly demeanour, Olaf Claussen came over to join their conversation, playfully slapping Julius on the back before firmly shaking his hand. He wanted to make a fresh start with everything, and that included his relationship with Julius.

"Good to see you, Julius, this wonderful Danish food is making me feel quite homesick already! How is the business going? Getting settled?"

Once his initial questions were answered he moved along to introduce himself to the Chairman, who he viewed as a potentially valuable contact and a person of influence.

Julius was anxious to return his attention to Agnes and cast his eyes upon her once again. Her head was tilted back as she poured an oyster into her mouth, direct from its whitish grey shell. A trickle of liquor ran down her chin which he deftly dabbed with his napkin. It was a simple gesture, though an intimate one in the circumstances. He felt so comfortable in her presence that it had happened quite spontaneously. She laughed and her eyes were dancing. He eagerly wanted to know if she still experienced their special connection, which to him was ever tangible. He decided he would put her to the test.

"Agnes, I am thinking of an object. I am focusing on an image in my mind. I want you to tell me what it is".

After half a minute of concentration she confidently replied, "It's a blue bible... embossed with a silver cross".

Julius nodded slowly, a smile spread over his face, and in unison they exclaimed, Two minds, a single thought!"

The midwest became a popular area for immigrants. A rapid influx of settlers came and the population increased which dramatically improved the local economy. Missouri became an important trading centre; with expansion of railroads from the west, and travel along the Mississippi river it soon became an economic hotspot. The largest number of Danish immigrants established themselves in Wisconsin in the 1880's and it is to this heavily concentrated Danish community that the Jorgensens and later, the Claussens were attracted. A major iron mining area at this time was the Gogebic Iron Range and the new discovery of widespread deposits shifted the focus to Northern Wisconsin.

It was no coincidence that the families set up their homes in the same county. Julius's father, Anton, was a close friend of Olaf Claussen and had tried to persuade him to join the immigration drift. Olaf's initial resistance to the idea gradually softened as his financial status weakened. He became increasingly interested in land opportunities; the vast open spaces and the chance to build a large, farming homestead tempted him. Anton wrote to him from Missouri, describing his new life; other settlers began writing letters to Danish newspapers, extolling the virtues of the new land and encouraging others to follow. The vision of a richer lifestyle became clearer to Olaf and he began to make the necessary plans to relocate his family to that same region. He decided it would be helpful to go to a place with some familiar faces in order to make business contacts. He had a hunch that he would soon be living his own 'American Dream'.

Olaf was not a man of strong religious belief but he needed to meet people and strike deals if he were to make a success of himself.

He saw the First Baptist Church as a good place to frequent, seeking acceptance into the neighbourhood and wishing ultimately to be recognised as *a pillar of the community*.

The Claussens went along to church, joining up with the Jorgensens and Pastor Peterson welcomed them all into the congregation. Julius and Agnes were delighted at the prospect of seeing each other every Sunday which was a convenient arrangement and something to look forward to. Agnes's mother Ida watched her daughter selecting her best clothes, suspecting this was not so much in honour of God but rather for Julius's delectation. Ida was fond of Julius, knowing him to be polite and perceiving him to be hard working. She felt there was something special about the young man, now aged twenty eight; she thought how charismatic he was, a little theatrical, even. Agnes was just twenty years old, though mature and pragmatic which helped to reduce their age difference. Ida decided they were a good match, despite being all too aware of Olaf's misgivings. What will be, will be, she thought as Agnes secured her raffia bonnet with a long hat pin. They were now ready to make the journey by horse and buggy to church.

The following week something special was going to happen. There would be an immersion baptism service which would, in part, take place at the river. First they would listen to the sermon in the church, sing hymns of praise and say prayers. The congregation would then file down the aisle to music from the pipe organ, then trek the short distance to the river bank. Agnes had never witnessed such a thing as this but Julius had already attended a couple of services and knew what to expect. He had a strong feeling that Agnes would have to suppress a fit of giggles and tried to prepare her for the bizarre sight.

Pastor Peterson waded waist deep into the water, his gown flowing behind him until it became saturated and dragged beneath the surface. Following behind the Pastor was an assistant and the four men who presented themselves to be baptised. Once they were all in position the Pastor's voice boomed out,

"We believe in a holy Christian church, the communion of saints, the resurrection and life everlasting. We are here to witness this special moment on the journey of faith. It is a moment when God's presence and blessing meets us, and when we make our personal commitment of faith in Jesus Christ our Lord. I will ask each one of you in turn to make your Confession of Faith before the congregation and before God, then you shall be symbolically cleansed and immersed in the waters that were God's first blessed creation".

Julius had been watching Agnes closely. He could see her eyes were wide and her mouth slightly open, in awe. Each man was grasped around his upper body by the pastor and his ceremonial assistant, then the willing participant was tipped backwards and fully submerged in the river water.

"I baptise you in the name of the Father, the Son and the Holy Spirit", said Pastor Peterson, four times over. The sight of the bedraggled party plodging from the river was too much for Agnes who feigned a coughing fit in an attempt to cover up her amusement.

Once the crowd had dispersed she looked Julian in the eye and asked, "What am I thinking?"

"Without reading your mind, you are thinking that's the strangest thing you've seen and you thought it quite hilarious?" he answered.

"I was actually thinking that Pastor Peterson's sandals are going to take a while to dry out and the leather will be ruined!" she laughed. Arm in arm they headed back to the church, following in the wet trail of footprints mapped out before them.

The following Sunday was fairly mundane in comparison. Proceedings followed in conventional style with the regular hymns and prayers. One thing was different though; there was entertainment provided by Lars Christensen, a violinist who had also emigrated from Denmark a couple of decades before. He was part of a travelling orchestra that performed in dance halls and at social functions and his moving concerto was enjoyed by everyone. Before bringing the service to a close, Pastor Peterson asked if any of the congregation could play an instrument, sing, or provide entertainment of any variety.

He wanted to make his services lively and find different ways of honouring the Lord. Neither could play an instrument as such, though Julius was able to make a saw 'sing' producing some warbling, mournful sounds. He came up with a completely different idea which was definitely entertaining. Julius and Agnes weren't sure if what they had in mind would be suitable but they thought it would be fun to give it a try.

Julius quite often had sensory experiences and feelings that he could not explain. Sometimes things happened that seemed to be more than a coincidence. He might just look at someone in the distance and then that person would turn around and meet his eyes. On one occasion he had a premonition of an impending, tragic accident. First came a feeling of dread and foreboding. The disturbing vision that occurred in a wakeful state was of his Uncle Erik in the throes of an accident at his saw mill on the outskirts of Copenhagen. Whilst trying to free a jammed piece of wood from the stacker pile his hand became trapped in the mechanism. The blades of the saw stuttered spontaneously into action, severing his hand and causing his death from severe haemorrhage. There was no logical explanation for this horrific precognition and Julius didn't disclose it to anyone. When the accident actually occurred and news of it spread through his family he was truly shocked, not only at the loss of his relative in traumatic circumstances, but that his premonition had become a reality. There were other instances where vivid scenes played out in his mind, almost like dreams, though in a state of wakefulness. He wondered if he was mentally unwell and began to do some research. He suspected that he was experiencing symptoms of an extra sensory perception, though he dared not share with anyone other than Agnes, his self diagnosis.

Another consideration was that he may be clairvoyant. He certainly felt that he had an awareness of unknown or special objects without any prior knowledge. When Anton lost his pocket watch Julius was able to tell him it had slipped down behind a drawer and was hidden at the bottom of the tall boy. He had not seen it drop and did not find it there by chance but merely experienced a *sense of knowing and seeing it in his mind*. Initially this was disturbing to Julius but then he began to consider how it could be usefully applied. The more he thought about it the more intrigued by its potential he became.

To meet Agnes and discover that similar things had happened to her was a pleasing and comforting revelation.

Agnes admitted that she first sensed a special connection with a lady friend. She explained to Julius that on the same day and without any prior discussion they exchanged scarves of identical design with each other. Initially this seemed to be just coincidence but other things happened for which no rational explanation could be found. Now she felt strongly connected to Julius, not solely in a romantic way, but in a cerebral way. Sometimes she experienced feelings of intuition or sixth sense. It seemed that she and Julius shared an extraordinary skill of thought transference. They invented and practiced a variety of thought agility and acuity *tasks* to strengthen their channels of communication. It was unclear to them at this time how these skills might be employed, other than for their own entertainment. They would wait and watch for a sign to present itself, and allow the hand of fate to direct them.

In Copenhagen the summer months are fairly warm and the long school break is taken between June and August. As soon as Agnes had completed her chores she set off to see Julius at the iron smelting plant. She prepared lunch for them and walked the fairly lengthy distance to his work place. On arrival she waited at the wide, slanted tree stump for Julius to take his lunch break. Even though he was ravenous she would make him visualise the produce of the food hamper and invariably he would correctly state its contents.

"Today you have brought...let me think..medister (spiced sausage) followed by... ebelskeiver pancakes". This was not the most reliable of tests due to the lack of variety of ingredients and Agnes's limited creativity. They ate and then took out the cards they had purposely designed to test each other's powers. The cards bore an assortment of shapes, colours and numbers. One of them would be the 'sender' who would view the randomly selected cards and try to telepathically communicate the symbol to the other. The receiver then tried to determine the correct card and announce it to the sender. Sometimes, Agnes would try to guess but then she found a way to banish all thoughts to make her mind a complete blank. In this passive state she discovered that she could receive 'thought pictures'. They were both capable of scoring six or seven out of ten correct images which they considered to be a higher than average success rate.

Julius began to explore other methods to try to improve his psychic abilities; one such technique was known as *scrying*. He began to concentrate on reflective, luminescent surfaces in order to 'see' messages or signs. He turned his attention to a variety of different textures and objects such as water reflection, stones and crystals. Sometimes he would stare into the pitch-black sky, trying to determine shapes in light patterns, in shadows and clouds. As his interest deepened he tried to remove unwanted thoughts from his mind and trained himself to be totally relaxed. He found he was able to chant a mantra which could induce in him a hypnotic trance.

He came to the realisation that his mind was incredibly receptive to such techniques. At this stage of his life he had no idea of its importance or relevance, but he was fully aware that Agnes had similar, mentalist potential and who knew where it might lead them.

Anton began more seriously discussing his thoughts of emigrating and the desire to increase his earning potential. He sensed that there were far greater opportunities in America than could be realised in Denmark. Times were changing even in different parts of Denmark and the feelings of repression became increasingly stifling. The cost of the voyage ticket for three of them was exorbitant, but he would use his life savings and sell their home and land to secure the necessary funds. For Julius and Agnes the radical plans should have caused apprehension and gloom and yet, this was not the case. They each had an innate feeling in their hearts and minds that this was not an end but the beginning of a new chapter. It was inexplicable that they should feel this way, as Olaf believed that he and his family would remain loyal to their homeland with no foreseeable intention to uproot. However, just ten months later the Claussen family had sold up and were en route, first destination, New York, then onwards to Missouri.

Julius and Anton worked very hard to establish themselves at the Missouri iron smelting plant. The work was very physically demanding and the environment presented its own challenges in terms of fumes, noisy vibration and excessive heat. Throughout all of Anton's years as foundryman he accepted that the work was hazardous, even unhealthy, but it had become a way of life that he no longer questioned. Julius had reached the end of his apprenticeship and began to feel uneasy about spending the rest of his working life in a hot hell hole. More and more he felt the irony of living in Missouri with its flat prairie plains, rivers and caves that he so wanted to explore. His desire to roam the forested ridges, to enjoy the fresh air and to camp beneath the stars began to take a greater hold. A feeling of being caged, trapped by the demands of working at the smelting plant increasingly gnawed at him. He planned an imaginary trip where he would see bison, mountain lions and watch the swooping peregrine falcons in the wild. He was happily daydreaming and not applying the rule of 'safety first' that Anton had drilled into him. Suddenly some molten metal splattered up from the iron cast, spraying and sizzling the skin of his forearm and hand. The pain was instant and agonising as he rushed to the water butt to immerse his arm. The cool water offered only very temporary relief and the upper layers of skin instantly wrinkled and sloughed, exposing raw flesh beneath. A co-worker rushed to his aid, covered the wound and led shocked Julius outside.

Anton came to see what all the fuss was about, initially shouting at his son and demanding to know why he hadn't been wearing arm guards.

Then, seeing Julius was so pale and agonised, he became more sympathetic. He knew how easily such accidents could happen, the molten medium was be unpredictable in its composition. It was a dreadful thing to happen, and meant that Julius would be unable to continue working for the next few weeks, or even months. Julius was wracked with pain and locked into the moment. In the days that followed he would reflect on and re-evaluate his position here, and decide what he really wanted to do. He surely wasn't destined to be a foundryman for the rest of his days.

With time on his hands he began to consider what else he might like to do, rather than what was expected of him. He became absorbed in subjects that fascinated him such as divination, palmistry, fortune telling and clairvoyance. He was drawn to things of an occult nature. He and Agnes discussed their future and how, together, they might harness their special, unique talents. They practiced their mentality tests and it was then that Julius suggested they should devise an act and that the congregation of The Baptist Church would be their first audience.

Julius decided he would discuss with Pastor Peterson what he and Agnes were planning to do, in light of not singing or playing an instrument. Some members of the congregation had recited poetry, played piano, strummed guitar or told jokes. Amos Whittaker's magic tricks had been well enough received. Julius was concerned that their mentalist act could cause offence if it were perceived as sinful or a transgression against God. The Pastor took a liberal stance, saying that people should be open-minded about things which could not be explained. The bible describes incredible events on which Christians form their beliefs, so he and Agnes should go ahead without fear of reprisal. He said he was looking forward to seeing them in church on Sunday, and it would soon be their turn to be centre stage.

A dull Sunday was about to be very much livened up and Pastor Peterson was surprised to see a few new faces in his congregation. After the service Julius and Agnes waited for the time to debut their act. Agnes was terribly nervous and had to be persuaded to go through with it. She whispered to Julius, telling him she didn't think she could go ahead with it after all.

"Agnes, you know how good we are! We must stick to our script, concentrate on our signals and clues and we will astonish our audience. Let's try and have fun and if we make mistakes they might think it's part of the act!" Julius said, then taking both of her hands in his, and looking into her eyes he continued, "I will introduce us and the audience will soon be eager to participate. Take some deep breaths, now follow me!"

They both stood on stage in front of a plain canvas backdrop, then Julius began.

"Ladies and Gentlemen, I'm delighted to introduce to you our unique, two-person mentalism act which we are certain will delight and astound you all. I will ask for certain items to be offered by yourselves so that my lovely assistant, Agnes, heavily blindfolded, will use her telepathic powers to name any given object! I promise you that she will be able to correctly identify any article, number or word that is presented to me. Now, for your entertainment and amazement I ask that you welcome Miss Agnes Claussen!" There was a burst of hearty applause as Agnes bobbed a bashful courtesy to the audience.

Julius passed the black velvet blindfold to a member of the audience and to Pastor Peterson. "Can you please confirm that the material is sufficiently thick that no light or shapes or indeed, *anything* can be seen through the fabric?" and once they both nodded in agreement he wrapped it around Agnes's forehead, ensuring that her eyes were fully covered.

Then he ventured into the audience.

"Please could I take that object from you, just for a moment, and hold it in my hand. Agnes will demonstrate that she can read my mind when she correctly identifies what I am holding.

"Agnes, what do I hold in my hand?" he asked, and waited for a few seconds for her response. "Please tell us what you see. Agnes is concentrating very hard, please be patient while our wavelengths connect".

"You are holding a pair of spectacles!" announced Agnes, and a gasp from the audience rippled around the room.

"That is correct! Can you describe in more detail, the spectacles?"

"They belong to a gentleman and are horn-rimmed in design," declared Agnes, and again there were exclamations of surprise and delight.

"There is a small crack in the left lens", she added.

The owner shouted, "No, there is no crack", and then to his surprise he noticed the flaw for the first time. "I was wrong, that's astonishing, the young lady is quite right!" he declared, shaking his head in disbelief.

"Now, concentrate on what I see", said Julius, as he was offered a fan by one of the ladies. "Can we allow Agnes a few seconds to read my mind and describe to us this second article?"

"There is no doubt that you hold a black fan, I believe, of oriental design", said Agnes.

"Can you tell us anything else of the design?" asked Julius

"I see a peacock!"

Then Julius moved quickly on as the excitement mounted.

"Now tell me what lies in my palm?" Julius was presented with a little silver charm by a very enthusiastic lady, eager to participate.

"This time you have something made of a light metal… in the shape of an animal…an elephant…I think…yes it is…a silver elephant!" stated Agnes.

"Next, can you please identify this item?" Julius held a small coin and waited.

" I have a vision of a coin," said Agnes.

"Can you be any more specific, I ask? replied Julius.

"It's a five cent piece!" she stated confidently.

"You see, everyone, it's truly amazing! Let us identify one more thing before we move to something different. Oh, Agnes, do you read the year of issue of that coin, please?"

"Yes, I can tell you exactly...that it is dated 1883, a Liberty Head nickel!"

By now the church was in uproar with people shouting and expressing their disbelief, or sheer fascination. It was exactly the zestful reaction that Julius had hoped for.

"Thank you for your participation, dear audience! I will now open a hymn book at a certain page and ask Agnes to reveal not only the page number but the title of the hymn on that same page. Which pages am I holding open? Please may I ask what you see?"

"Pages forty one and page forty two. Firstly, Rock of Ages....and then Jesus, Lover of my Soul!"

"Now, I would ask if one of you could write your date of birth on a piece of paper, and pass it to me". Julius was handed the sheet, and he studied it hard.

"Agnes, I am asking you to think carefully and to fixate. Could you furnish us with the information written on this paper?"

"The date of birth is scribed as July thirtieth, 1839".

"That is, indeed, correct, and magnificently detected!" cried Julius, and there were people shouting, cheering and applauding their success.

"Well, wasn't that something!" exclaimed Pastor Peterson to his astonished congregation. "I've never seen the like of it before and I'm sure you will all say the same. How do they do it? I really have no idea how it's possible! Can we show our appreciation to Julius and Agnes for entertaining us in such a captivating way".

Even though it was not the polished performance he was aiming for, Julius was delighted at how the act was received. He knew they could perfect it, make it amusing and introduce new ideas to keep it fresh. He noticed the brightness of Agnes's eyes, her flushed skin and beaming smile. "I told you we could do it!" he said, grasping her by the waist and swinging her around. He wondered where the act might take them, but more importantly, how he could persuade Agnes to stay with him.

In the days that followed, everyone talked of only one thing. On street corners, at the grocery store, in the saloon, they were all asking the question, 'how do they do it?'. There were many different theories from the supporting believers, and other disparaging comments from those who were unconvinced of the act's credibility. Julius was delighted that they had caused such a sensation and revelled in the attention that came their way. It was matterless to him whether they believed in telepathy or not. Curiosity and a desire to find flaws or to celebrate the success of the act is all he hoped for. If they were able to attract numbers, get bookings and, dare he think, make a living from the act, that would be a marvellous thing. Suddenly the couple became popular, being invited to entertain at dinner parties and to give private readings in the evenings. A small amount of money was generated and proved that there was a niche for this enterprise.

Julius needed to explore if Agnes would join him, because without her he was nothing. He did a lot of thinking in the following days and considered those few words, turning them over and over in his head. *Without Agnes, I am nothing.* Her father would certainly not approve of the venture. He must propose to Agnes and hope that she will agree to marry him in secret, then they will be free to go where they please. No-one and nothing would be able to stop them. *Agnes, the world will be our oyster, if you will just say yes,* he thought.

Julius had no intention of returning to his work at the iron smelting plant. His burns were slowly healing but it had been a long, painful process which would leave him with scarred tissue. He had been taking prescribed medication to ease the pain and a side effect of the drugs caused Julius to hallucinate. Sometimes in the transitional state of wakefulness and falling to sleep he experienced premonitions. One such situation was that he and Agnes were on the road, travelling between venues. The coach and horses that carried them had to stop in the middle of the road as people swarmed around, engulfing them and obstructing the way ahead. They were all brandishing dollar bills in their fists and mobbing them for show tickets. Whilst this premonition alluded to future success, in contrast he experienced some frightening visions of jumping from a cliff top not daring to look down as he worked out how to fly. This felt like a harbinger of doom or warning of possible failure, a feeling he must disregard and overcome. He was determined to succeed and spent every moment thinking about how he could make the act work. He read books on fortune telling and the occult and became obsessed with how a combination of themes could augment the act.

Some of the anxieties he experienced were related to what might happen if Agnes should turn him down, decline his marriage proposal and what would happen then. It was something he must address. So a plan began to formulate and he decided to pawn a pocket watch that was gifted to him by his parents for his twenty first birthday. He felt so sure that he would make enough money in order to buy it back in the near future. A ring for Agnes is what he really needed and must acquire right now. It seemed to him to be the most important thing and a fine starting point to get the show on the road.

In a field of corn maize, on a day when the cirrus clouds scuttled across the sky, they gazed up at the evolving shapes.

"Agnes, I have something important to ask you", Julius began. She turned onto her side and anxiously tried to gauge his expression.

Julius turned to meet her gaze. "I was thinking of you the other day. Well, I actually think of you every day! I want you to know how much you mean to me...I feel that I am nothing without you. When I saw you again that first time at the welcome meeting, my heart.. sang".

"Oh, dear Julius, she said, and touched his face tenderly. "I felt the same about you. I didn't realise how much I missed you until you were right before me again".

"Agnes, I think you know the question that I dearly wish to ask?"

"Yes, yes, but please ask it anyway", she said playfully.

"Agnes, I love you and I would be honoured if you would accept my hand in marriage. I promise to always take care of you."

And at the moment she accepted his proposal he began rambling," Are you sure we can continue with our act? Make it the most amazing thing that we can for our audience, practice until it's seamless, even flawless? Travel with me, we will see the world and become rich and famous. I can't do it without you".

"From now on, where you go, I go", she assured him, laughing as Julius kissed away her tears of joy.

Pastor Peterson agreed to marry them in a private service with only themselves and two witnesses present . The service was arranged to take place on the first day of August, 1886. Julius wore the one and only suit he possessed. Agnes wore her favourite dress and decorated her hair with a fresh flower garland. It was a simple ceremony designed to meet their bare requirements, and only when their marriage was made legal did they inform their parents and friends. Olaf and Ida were shocked and initially disappointed at not being present. Ida especially felt hurt to have been denied the chance to fulfil her role as Mother of the Bride. It was too late to voice any concerns that Julius did not have a steady job and there were no plans for where they would settle or any other number of problems that might befall them. They were all too aware that this was most likely the reason why it had happened in such a secretive way, to avoid disagreement or conflict, but what could they do about it? They decided that they would give the couple their blessing and hope that it turned out positively for them. Agnes was too precious to them to be denied their love and support.

Anton was not foolish enough to believe that Julius was cut out for hard manual work at the foundry in the long term. His son was a fanciful dreamer with ambitions of travelling and entertaining. He had a lot to prove if he were to make a success of himself in that line of work but at least he had a trade to fall back on.

Word of Julius and Agnes's unusual act spread rapidly, not only locally but further afield. When news of it reached an influential theatrical producer he showed interest. He contacted Julius to suggest they strike a business deal, enabling their act to be showcased at the Michigan State Fair in the fall. The event was an annual, competitive gathering and a larger version of a local country fair. State fairs began in the nineteenth century initially to promote agriculture, to exhibit livestock and farm produce. Prize money was awarded to the finest examples of oxen, swine and sheep but the fairs soon began to incorporate musical entertainment and carnival rides. Fair-goers would be treated to a diverse range of things such as reenactments of Custer's Last Stand, tight-rope walking and displays of giant vegetables. Thousands of people attended the fair each day and from all walks of life so it was an amazing opportunity to be seen.

A small stage area was purpose built and they performed several times a day to the eagerly waiting crowds. In these early days Julius introduced their act as *'Mister Julius Jorgensen and Mrs Agnes Jorgesen, Masters of Mentalism and Mind Reading"* and their skilled demonstrations caused curiosity and wonderment to all. As their fame and popularity grew they styled themselves, adopting the stage name of *Professor and Madame Zancig, or The Zancigs.* The crowds kept on coming and spreading the word all around the fairground. No one could fathom how the act worked and they were utterly convinced that psychic or supernatural forces were employed. They questioned if it was due to subliminal communication, expert analysis of body language or higher emotional intelligence but there were no answers. Agnes became increasingly confident in her ability to correctly identify objects and to astonish their audiences. The pair worked swiftly and accurately, accepting all challenges that were presented to them, deflecting any attempts by the crowd to confuse or baffle them. They became an overnight sensation and soon were headhunted for the Sans Souci Amusement Park at Chicago, Illinois.

Julius was constantly thinking about how he could augment the act, looking at other things that he could incorporate such as illusions, mechanical, magical effects and manual dexterity tricks. He became aware of the work of another couple, Robert and Haidee Heller, illusionists and creators of the Second Sight Act. Haidee was billed as Robert's sister but was thought to be his mistress. Haidee sat upon a sofa while Robert held up hidden objects for her to correctly identify. There were a few other performers at this time presenting acts of a similar nature, all of which were the subject of curiosity. Newspapers occasionally printed exposures, claiming that code words were used, but in the absence of dialogue, audiences and magicians alike were dumbfounded. Even though they did not speak a word, Haidee knew the answers to various questions or was able to reveal hidden objects. Many years passed before it was revealed that the sofa was filled with wires and a battery which ran off stage to a hidden assistant. A secret 'plant' in the audience had an electric button under his seat and could tap out a coded signal to the occupant of the couch. It was an example of how magicians used the latest advances in science to create their illusions. For the Zancigs there were no wires, optical projections or smoke screen trickery. They worked extremely hard and practised every day to achieve the highest level of showmanship, for Julius was a perfectionist and he expected the same of Agnes.

Sans Souci opened in the summer of 1899 as one of Chicago's first amusement parks it was advertised as *The Most Beautiful Amusement Park in America.* The new ten acre park was named after the famous palace of Prussian King Frederick the Great and was unlike anything Chicagoans had ever seen. The main entrance resembled the exterior of a German beer hall. Inside the park there was a Japanese tea garden, electric fountains and night time lighting. A popular attraction was the casino and a large space for al fresco dining whilst listening to bands and orchestras. Finest cuisine and unexcelled service were promised along with the almost up to date shows, the classiest bands and longest, safest rides. One of the ride attractions was The Bear Cat roller coaster, a tall wooden structure designed to thrill and terrify.

Most notably the park incorporated the best Vaudeville Music Hall and Electric Theatre. Vaudeville was made up of an eclectic range of performers such as comedians, plate spinners and ventriloquists. There was a gathering of astrologers, palmists and fortune tellers of all varieties and this provided the first big break for the Zancigs. They were contracted for only one season, on a percentage basis of the takings and proved to be very popular. Julius's request for more money was refused, so there was no second season. The Zancigs decided to concentrate on their private engagements where there was much greater earning potential.

One of these last performances was attended by the impresario Oscar Hammerstein who offered them $1,500 a week to play at his Roof Garden in New York for eleven weeks. The semi-outdoor vaudeville venue was built on top of the Victoria Theatre and the neighbouring Belasco Theatre. The rooftop area accommodated summer performances as there was no air conditioning at the turn of the century many theatres had to close. It later became known as The Paradise Roof Garden and attracted such acts as Barnold's Dog and Monkey Pantomime Company and Wire Walking Man Bird Millman. The Barrison Sisters were a risque act, billed as The Wickedest Girls in the World. The five blonde haired siblings sang in high, squeaky voices and achieved notoriety through use of double entendres on stage. They would perform a provocative, cat dance, gradually raising their skirts until the conclusion of the act where they each revealed a kitten stitched into their knickers!

The unity that existed between Julius and Agnes manifested itself in a variety of ways. Agnes would repeatedly mention events that Julius was thinking about but had not spoken. Things happened which could not be accounted for, with Agnes merely stating *that she just saw it.* Having become proficient in the art of thought transference they used this novelty form of entertainment to astound their friends. One day a friend was visiting their apartment when Julius announced that he needed to pick up a parcel from a shop. He would only be gone for the short time it would take to make the journey on foot. While he was away, Agnes commented to the friend that something had happened to Julius, that he had sustained an accident to his foot. The friend thought this was very strange and questioned how Agnes could possibly know such a thing. When Julius limped in, explaining he had slipped off a kerb and sprained his ankle, the friend was incredulous at the accurate prediction. On another occasion, Julius was thinking of a Gladstone bag that he would like to buy and the next day, Agnes gifted the very same article to him. Duplicate theatre tickets were purchased by the pair with the lady in the box office remarking that one or the other had already made the booking. There were many, similar incidents that were proof of their closeness and shared thoughts.

The Zancigs were the act that most wanted to see and the exposure they gained at the Roof Garden led to many lucrative, high society functions. It was during this time that they really became famous.

Following a twelve week stint at the prestigious Waldorf Astoria Hotel they were headhunted by the theatrical producer H.B Leavitt. He was so impressed by their polished performances and professionalism that he offered to arrange a globetrotting tour beginning at The Alhambra Theatre of Variety in London, England.

The curtain was raised, revealing to another full house 'Madame and Professor Zancig', who were by now the most well known mentalism act. Julius stood in the middle of the stage, dressed in a white 'tropics' suit, which it was claimed, made it easier to see his hands. Agnes wore a simple flowered hat and high necked Victorian dress which draped to the floor. With her back to the audience she held a slate and piece of chalk to record transmitted messages. At other times she was blindfolded, and so began the routine of describing all manner of exhibits that were presented to Julius. In the early days such regular items as spectacles, monogrammed handkerchiefs and charms were to be expected. Now the audience would bring their obscure items such as half a lemon, a jewelled dagger, a piece of hangman's rope and even a live tortoise. Long Welsh words that were too difficult to pronounce would be offered for translation, specific book passages and arithmetic equations were all correctly identified to astonished audiences. No test proved too difficult and every member of the audience left with so many questions, trying to fathom the secrets of the Zancigs. Was it a natural ability, did they read each other's body language, did they engage in subliminal communication or possess a higher emotional intelligence? There were so many questions and simply no answers but the crowds kept coming and the money continued to roll in. Even the Zancigs felt they had exceeded their wildest expectations when they were invited by King-Emperor Edward the Seventh to perform at one of his royal estates.

On a snowy evening in December 1906, a royal coach was waiting at the train station to transport them to his country home of Sandringham. They were surprised to see quite a crowd of people gathered there to greet them. The couple were nervous at the prospect of what lay ahead but on arrival were treated like royalty themselves by the servants who received them. They gave an impromptu show below stairs, to the delight of the staff. In the saloon drawing room the smiling King greeted them in such a friendly manner that they soon felt at ease. The room was grandly decorated with wooden panelling and ornate columns, overlooked from above by a minstrel's gallery. He introduced to them his wife, Queen Alexandra who also hailed from Denmark and they were encouraged to converse together in Danish. Also present were the Prince and Princess of Wales.

The scene was set for them to demonstrate their marvellous powers and Agnes was concealed behind a decorative, Japanese screen. The young princess kept Agnes in full view, ensuring there was no deception or collusion. The King suggested they should begin the entertainment and randomly selected a difficult passage from a scientific book. The ease and speed that Julius was able to convey the passage to Agnes astounded the royals. Then the word 'Cagliostro' was written down, which Agnes spoke of without a moment's hesitation, to their wonderment and delight. Neither of them were familiar with the word and later discovered it to be the name of an Italian adventurer and magician. Queen Alexandra wrote,' En Gliedetig Jul', which translated, meant, 'A merry Christmas' as Julius visualised the words, Agnes spoke them in their native tongue, much to the pleasure of Her Majesty. Next came a revelation from a catalogue selected by the King, as Julius was able to transfer the fact that it erroneously had two pages that were numbered 'six'. When the King drew a rough sketch of his yacht Agnes was able to replicate this picture using chalk on a slate. A racing diary containing a long list of Derby winners was produced and Agnes described these particulars as if reading from the pages of a newspaper. It was no small test to convey the name of the horse and jockey, as well as the date and time in which the race was run. When they had passed every conceivable test that was set, their Majesties were most interested in their methods, asking all manner of questions. Queen Alexandra wanted to know if they would ever share the secret of how their feats were accomplished. Julius replied, "Your Majesty, I most humbly apologise, but that is one piece of information I am not at liberty to divulge to anyone. I trust you will understand and forgive me".

The rest of the evening was rather more relaxing, with great hospitality being offered by the royal party and a delicious supper set out for them. They stayed the night in a sumptuous bed chamber and in the morning were shown all over the house, feasting their eyes on the wrapped Christmas presents.

The Zancigs were a sensation in London; they toured across England as they had done once before, maintaining their 'top of the bill' status at The Orpheum Theatre and all other music hall venues. In a 1906 issue of The Conjurers Monthly magazine, Houdini wrote, "Their act is the best of its kind that we have ever seen, and we have seen almost all! Their exhibition may be termed telepathy, mind reading, second sight, or by any other name. It goes just the same". They travelled to The Winter Gardens, Germany, then embarked on a world tour to include India, China, Australia and South Africa before returning to America. They were heralded as 'Master Mystics of Five Continents,' a high accolade indeed.

Still, there were no answers for the cynics and the skeptics as to how the Zancigs achieved such accuracy and precision. Scholars and educated audiences could not figure out their showmanship and bravado. They never claimed to harness occult powers despite both having published books and written articles for magazines on clairvoyance. Julius maintained that he and Agnes could account for their power on the grounds of a most happy union, perfect harmony and the development of a latent gift. In his 1907 book, "Two Minds But With a Single Thought", he implied that a psychic connection existed between them. They preferred, where possible, to leave it to others to explain their phenomenon. To the harsh cynics who declared the act as pure hokum, attributing their ability to a complex code, Julius would declare, "Yes, your guess may be right, but I leave it to you!"

They were so confident in their abilities that they agreed to undergo testing by leading psychologists and the Society for Psychical Research who were forever in pursuit of any supporting scientific evidence. During one such study, Agnes was seated behind a screen at the furthest end of the room. Two investigators held her hands and watched carefully to try to detect any means by which she could receive any sort of signal. A physician monitored her pulse and observed her for any flickering of the eyelids. Julius conveyed mental impressions of drawings on cards; one bore an ink blot which was designed to outwit them. Agnes was able to correctly identify the irregular ink shape. The Society for Psychical Research concluded that they found it hard to offer any plausible explanation for their clever and perplexing *modus operandi*.

In the autumn of 1915 the act was in ever high demand and ticket sales were booming, though Agnes began to struggle with the physical and mental demands of performing. They were at their pinnacle of fame and notoriety and despite a rise in the amount of copycat acts, none were considered to be in the same league. Julius began to reduce their appearances in order for Agnes to rest more and try to recuperate. They continued to fulfil some less demanding private functions, focusing on palmistry readings, astrology and crystal ball gazing. The lessened workload did not seem to improve things for Agnes who complained of increased fatigue, headaches and general malaise. Doctors could not find a specific problem or give a diagnosis and it was upsetting for Julius to watch her health deteriorate as winter approached. By spring of the following year Agnes was extremely debilitated, resting in bed for long periods and only managing to function on a very basic level. It seemed that nothing could be done to improve her health and she became a shadow of her former self as she battled with pneumonia. Julius was heartbroken as she slipped away from him on April 8th 1916.

It is a sad irony that the couple did not foresee the tragedy that lay ahead when Agnes became ill and that she would not have the strength to recover. Julius lost his lifelong love and partner when she died and he expressed his love for Agnes in a small booklet that he titled, 'Adventures in Many Lands'. The book insisted on love as the foundation of the Zancigs' success. Julius wrote, "After thirty years of completely happy, married life my wife died. I thought that the end of everything had come to me. It seemed that there was nothing in life worth living for, without her.'

The act represented his life work to which he had dedicated all of his energies and devotion, making it a difficult thing for Julius to let go. He made several attempts to find new partners but never managed to achieve the same level of success on stage that he had with Agnes. The act could not continue; the dynamics were different, there was not the same rapport with the others. Eventually he withdrew from live appearances, concentrating on sittings with his wealthy, private clients. He lived out the rest of his days in Santa Monica, California, and as his own health began to decline, he took the huge decision to reveal the existence of their secret code. He sold the secrets of the code to a popular British weekly magazine, *'Answers'* confessing that the mentalist act was based on an extremely elaborate and complex verbal code that they had devised. The pioneering methods were so thorough that detection had been an impossibility, and many learned people had been fooled, including the spiritualist Arthur Conan Doyle. Through use of a framed question asked in a certain manner, any article, number or word could be communicated.

Each phrase was a coded clue, each word was most specifically chosen to convey a mutual message that described any article, number or word, "Madame, can you tell me...here what is this...now, Agnes, concentrate on this..."

They had never completely discounted the possibility of a unique, spiritual connection, which to them was true and real. Indeed, it is doubtful that any two highly receptive minds in history have been in the same, attuned thought vibration.

Julius offered the following advice to anyone wishing to emulate their wonderful achievements, "I should say to those who would develop the power: find your other half, the alter ego, the one person who is needed to bring complete harmony into your life. Then the rest is practice".

Their full methodology was eventually published by the Zancigs' friend and fellow mentalist-magician, 'Alexander the Crystal Seer' in 1929, following Julius's death at the age of seventy two.

To this day the Zancig Code is considered to be the most daunting, complex, two person communication of its type. This is not just a story of magic making, of travelling the world or of enduring career success. It is, of course, all of these things and more. The story of Julius and Agnes is testament to the couple's devotion, their emotional intelligence and love that they unquestionably shared, which none can claim was an illusion.

Further reading: See Wikipedia entry re Julius and Agnes Zancig

~~~~~~oOo~~~~~~